A Heart's Odyssey

The author and Marily on their wedding day

A Heart's Odyssey

Neil Macvicar

When you set out to go to Ithaca,
Pray that the road may be a long one.

C.P. CAVAFY

MICHAEL RUSSELL

© Neil Macvicar 1990

First published in Great Britain 1990
by Michael Russell (Publishing) Ltd
The Chantry, Wilton, Salisbury, Wiltshire
Typeset by Dave Sullivan Typesetting
Oakdale, Poole, Dorset
Printed and bound in Great Britain
by Biddles Ltd, Guildford and King's Lynn

ISBN 0 85955 171 7

For Marily

Contents

Prologue

Marily and I were married at the Saint – *ston Ayio,* as they say in Corfu. They mean, of course, in the church behind the Plateia, with the tall red-nightcapped bell tower, where their patron saint, Spyridion, lies in his silver casket and embroidered slippers, serenely awaiting the Last Trump.

It was the inevitable place for our wedding, given that the saint is almost one of Marily's family. His mortal remains (less one forearm, which had at one time been detached and was venerated in a church in Rome) came into it along with the sheets and pillow-cases and silver spoons of a dowry, and were cared for by a succession of family priests for four hundred years. By the time that I arrived in Corfu, rights of private property in a sacred relic had become unacceptable, and Saint Spyridion had been de-privatised. But Marily's grandfather, Papa Stephanos, still remained the priest of the church, and our nuptials would have been incomplete without the old miracle-worker to give us his blessing, from his shrine behind the marble *iconostasis.*

He must have been the only cool person present. It was the hottest day of a hot Greek summer. At six in the evening the high houses and narrow streets of the town were beginning to give back the heat that the sun had poured into them since dawn. In the oasis of the church the temperature was only relatively more bearable. Beneath the painted saints and angels on the ceiling and the hanging silver lamps and candelabra, the congregation was a-flutter with handkerchiefs and fans. Sweating in my kilt, with full rig of dress jacket and lace jabot, I began to think that the desire to create a romantic Scottish-Hellenic effect had been too much of a good thing.

The service was conducted not by Papa Stephanos, but by

9

the bishop's *protosyngelos,* the Archimandrite Chrysanthos. He was very fat and imposing and might, I suspect, have become a bishop himself if he had not suffered from the defect, serious in an Orthodox cleric, of not being able to sing in tune. The ceremony floated with Byzantine deliberation on the current of his monotone. The betrothal rings were placed on our fingers; the ribbon-linked wreaths of orange blossom were passed and re-passed above, and finally settled on, our heads; together we drank blessed wine from the marriage cup. At one point the lovely guileless girl at my side stood smartly and without warning on my toes, to let me know, according to an old Greek custom, which of us was to be the boss. Lastly, the *protosyngelos,* his beard foaming over the prow of his stomach, led us thrice round the table in Isaiah's dance, through a blatter of rice and rose petals.

It was a long way from my douce, Piskie,★ Edinburgh beginnings, but such is the spell of love that it all seemed most marvellously foreordained. Pure chance, reason says, that I was a subaltern in a regiment which happened to be handy in the south of Italy in December 1944, and could be diverted to war-riven Athens, Yet even now the solemnities at the Saint feel as if they were both the start of a new journey and the destined culmination of an old one, on which I had set out before I was aware of it.

★ i.e. Scottish Episcopalian, as in the Calvinist canticle:
  'Piskie, Piskie, Amen. Doon on yir knees and up again.'

One

It is a century and a half since Nathaniel Hawthorne, early in his literary career, published his versions of the better known Greek myths, under the title of *Tanglewood Tales*. An edition of this, illustrated in colour, is the first book I remember. To be accurate, I remember the pictures. I think that my mother (my father not being much of a man for myth) must have read the stories aloud to me, while my eye took in the white, garlanded bull-god carrying the girl Europa on his back into the sea, Cadmus' fierce little dragon-teeth soldiers, Odysseus' companions turned to pigs and rooting for acorns in Circe's oak wood, the black sails of Theseus' ships drawing nearer to his father's despairing gaze.

So the knapsack of my mind held, very early, some at least of the luggage which all ancient Greeks carried through life, which was the stuff of their poetry, painting and sculpture; and with which they peopled the starry sky.

I came into direct contact with Greek literature at the age of ten, when, on the strength of a precocious memory and clear diction, I was cast as the god Dionysus in a school production of *The Frogs* by Aristophanes. Naturally this was not in Greek, but in Gilbert Murray's translation, further bowdlerised so as not to bring a blush to the cheek of the young person. The plot required me to visit Hades, disguised as the hero Heracles, and to be rowed across the River Styx by Charon the ferryman. I was towed jerkily across the gymnasium floor in a mock boat, clad in the world's smallest lion skin, while a chorus of schoolfellows hopped round us, squeakily croaking, 'Brek-ek-ek-ex, koäx. (For years I supposed that this frog-noise had been invented by the poet, probably for metric reasons. Frogs on the whole seemed to speak indistinctly, except for the big ones in North Africa who, in the mating season, went 'In – out, in – out' like boat race radio commentators. Eventually, however, watching birds by the Korissia lagoon in Corfu, I heard a frog in the reeds use the very same words, with a crisp Athenian accent, and in the rhythm that Aristophanes caught for his chorus.)

The instigator and producer of this comically ambitious theatrical venture was our headmaster, Frank Wailes. He was a straightforward enthusiastic Yorkshireman, with a fondness for shooting pheasants. He owned the school, which he had started himself, and ran it on the principle that the foundations of a proper education are the three C's – classics, cricket and Christianity, preferably a moderate Anglicanism. He was, by today's standards, old-fashioned, but it would be unfair to deride him. He led us untiringly in the pursuit of excellence. The school motto – in Latin of course – was 'Altiora in corde disponamus', or, in plain English, 'Aim high'.

About the same time that I made my debut on the boards, Frank Wailes started a few of us to learn ancient Greek. He taught me my first Greek words in a sunny classroom, with high windows looking out over tennis courts and a copper beech tree to the muddy shore of the Forth estuary. They were, as one might expect, the definite article, singular number, nominative case, masculine, feminine and neuter genders. He wrote them on the blackboard, ὁ, ἡ, τό– 'hoe', 'he' and 'toe'. As he pronounced them they sounded reassuringly English, and would have baffled a modern Greek.

So I was off, pointed irrevocably in the direction of a classical education. More and more, over the next ten years, the language, literature and history of the Greeks and Romans became my main mental preoccupation. The Greek part was the best. To begin with, this had something to do with the feeling that we who learned Greek were a bit special. Everybody had to do Latin, but only we knew a language like a secret code, in an alphabet which the others could not read. Later it was because, in intellectual curiosity and artistic creativity, the Greeks left the Romans standing – indeed, it seemed unlikely that the Romans would have produced any worthwhile art without the example and inspiration of Greek civilisation.

I learned a lot about the ancient Greeks, especially those two or three remarkable generations who made Athens, in its glory, the school of all Hellas. I learned almost nothing at all about their descendants. We all knew what happened to the Romans. Their history flowed into that of Western Europe. One could even walk along the roads they had made and see the wall which they had built to keep our ancestors out of England. But the glory that was Greece was venerated in inverted commas, and was treated as having burned itself out when Philip of Macedon extinguished the liberty of the city-states. Those who taught me appeared to be uninterested in the achievements of Philip's stupendous son Alexander, or his successors in the Near and Middle East. Byzantium might have been a dirty word for all that we were told of it, and modern Greece was just another small, tiresome, backward Balkan state with a reputation for bad food and fleas in the inns.

Of all my teachers at school, only one to my knowledge had visited Greece, and he was not a classics master but a pale young man called Matthews who was hired as a stand-in to teach French, and who could be diverted from the exploits of Arsène Lupin to show us black-and-white picture postcards of the Acropolis and to speak a few words of the modern language. Nor were we urged to go and see Greece for ourselves. There was even one classical tutor I knew of who encouraged his students to spend their vacations not in Greece and Italy, but in Germany, the better to read Wilamo-witz-Moellendorf's commentaries on the Greek poets in the original German.

Such erudition was beyond me. I came to realise that

indolence, and a certain lightness of mind, unfitted me for a grammarian's funeral. Nevertheless, I drew increasing pleasure from the Greek poets, and from none more than Homer, the first and greatest of them all. I first read the whole of the *Odyssey* at the furthest end of Anglesey, staying with my friend Hugh. It was late June, and we used to spend the mornings reading in a Betjemanesque cliff-top world of short turf and sea-pinks, while the Irish Sea sucked its teeth forty feet below. It was there that I made the acquaintance of the sensible, good-hearted, ardent girl whom Homer had been in love with, and put in his poem, and called Nausicaa. Then we would clamber down to swim in little coves, with private names like Lavender and Lettice, after long-dead aunts, and finally, dazed with sun and salt, toil up the lane, scattering butterflies like confetti from the hedges, to the house where Mrs Roberts's vast country lunches awaited us. To this day the *Odyssey* carries with it, for me, a flavour of shepherd's pie and boiled onions.

Two months later the second German war began, and we went off, little by little, to be soldiers.

I spent the second winter of the war learning gunnery and trying not to catch my death of cold on Ilkley Moor. These activities kept one from brooding too deeply on the state of the war, which was not good. France had fallen, and almost all of central and north-western Europe were in German occupation. The Italians had joined what looked like the winning side, and were trying to extend their North African empire to include Egypt. The Russians, having assisted in the dismemberment of Poland and annexed the three independent Baltic states and part of Finland, were still linked to Germany by the Nazi-Soviet Pact of August 1939. (This infamous agreement had had the incidental effect of putting the British Communist Party on the side of the enemy, a state of matters which it appeared to accept with equanimity.)

Meanwhile, the night bombing of London – the Blitz – had begun. The evacuation of our men from Dunkirk and the Battle of Britain had summoned up the blood and perhaps used up too much adrenalin. Death screaming blindly out of a black sky was hard to take.

In the middle of all this, suddenly, Greece became a symbol of honour, pride and courage. On Easter Sunday 1939 Mussolini had sent his army marching into Albania. Now, a year and a half later, he presented the Greek government with a demand for certain territory in the north of Greece, claimed by the Albanians as theirs, and threatened to take it by force. The Greek dictator, Metaxas, answered the Italian dictator's impertinent ultimatum, speaking for the whole nation, with the single word 'No!', and Italy invaded. Nemesis succeeded hubris. The Greek army brought the advance to a halt, pushed the Italian forces back, and held them on the frontier throughout the winter of 1940/41. During those months almost the only cheerful news to come out of our wireless sets was the reports of the prodigies of Greek valour and endurance in the awful conditions of that mountain war. For the first time I saw the modern Greeks as real people and true heirs of the victors of the Battle of Marathon.

So Greece became one of the allies whose national anthems were played before the radio news on Sunday evenings. We came to know the music of Mantzaros which matched so well Solomos's stirring 'Hymn to Liberty'. No doubt the Metaxas regime was one we would have preferred not to be associated with, but neither then nor later did we require fellow fighters for freedom to pass examinations in parliamentary democracy. It was enough, and an inspiration, that for six months there was one country outside the Commonwealth with an army in the field against the aggression of the Berlin-Rome Axis.

It was too good to last of course. In the spring of 1941, Hitler, growing tired of the long-running Italian farce in the Albanian mountains and anxious to launch his treacherous attack on his Russian ally, sent Panzer divisions into Greece. We rushed what few troops we could spare – Australian, New Zealand and British – from the Middle East to help the Greek army, but within weeks it all ended in the Dunkirk-like evacuation from Crete. Greece followed our other allies into the tomb of German-occupied Europe.

At about this time I was posted to the artillery regiment (30th Field Regiment, RA) to which I was to belong for the next four and a half years. For most of that period I was a sub-altern in 112/117th Field Battery, commanded from 1941 to 1944 by Dick Cunliffe. He was a regular Gunner major of strong-minded eccentricity, with a passionate pride in, and loyalty to, his battery. He demanded and got a corresponding pride and loyalty from his officers, NCOs and men. The troop commanders and battery captain were also regular soldiers, but the junior officers were total amateurs like my-self (the major harboured an unreasonable prejudice against Territorials) and more or less of an age with me. It was a piece of good fortune to be able to learn one's soldiering, and to face the anxieties and boredom of war, within the support of such a society, and at the same time to make good friends.

Through the years, at first as part of the defence of the UK, and later in North Africa, Egypt and Italy, we did our best to survive and maintain a decent standard of living in the light of four basic maxims – probably no less useful in civilian life: 1 No bad soldiers, only bad officers; 2 Time spent in recon-naissance is never wasted; 3 Never get separated from your baggage; 4 Any fool can be uncomfortable. All these in-fluences played a part in making me what I was when eventually I came to Greece.

Greece, meanwhile, almost entirely disappeared from my consciousness for close on three years. There were plenty of other things to think about, and very little information trick-led out from behind the curtain of the occupation. One heard that there was a resistance movement, which we supported with men and supplies. It was possible to guess at the hardship which the andartes in the mountains were prepared to suffer. But it was not till after the liberation, years later, that one was able to piece together some of the realities of daily life for the mass of ordinary people in the cities and towns. In the winter of 1941 food was so short that many died of starvation in the streets of Athens. Less dramatic scarcity persisted throughout the whole three and a half years.

Basic foodstuffs such as meat, butter and sugar were rarely obtainable, except at high prices on the black market. Bread was made from a kind of flour of milled chick-peas, and acorns were ground to form a substitute for coffee. Marily was still at school during the occupation, living with her mother, two younger brothers and sister in an Athens suburb. They were able to supplement their diet by keeping hens, and an uncooperative goat named Josette, while Marily's mother sold some of her carpets and jewellery for the illicit gold which was the only acceptable currency for under-the-counter transactions. Even so, hunger was poorly assuaged. Marily used to dream, as the heart's dearest luxury, of thick slices of white bread, spread with butter from a real cow.

Resistance movements came into being early in the occupation. The largest, and increasingly the best known, was the Greek Liberation Front – known from its Greek initials as EAM – with its military wing, the Greek Popular Liberation Army, or ELAS. EAM/ELAS had cells in Athens and other towns, but its main fighting force consisted of guerrilla bands, the andartes, which operated principally in the mountains. The Allied Command in the Mediterranean supported ELAS with supplies of gold, arms and ammunition, which were either dropped by parachute or flown in to remote air strips. Officers and men, mostly British, were also infiltrated into Greece, to maintain contact between the andartes and the theatres of operations in North Africa and

Italy and to coordinate acts of sabotage against the occupying forces. These men shared the hard and dangerous life of the mountain fighters.

With time it became more and more obvious that EAM/ELAS were controlled by KKE, the Communist Party of Greece. They devoted a substantial part of their time, energies and resources to the elimination of any resistance groups of a different political persuasion, and established a virtual monopoly of military force which put the Communists in a strong position for achieving their long-term aim. This was, naturally, to take over Greece, as soon as possible after the German army had left the country.

As a result, EAM/ELAS became feared and hated by those Greeks who had no wish to live under a Communist regime. To begin with, however, this political slant was not publicised and the patriotic appeal of the movement drew young people from all walks of society to join or at least to support it. Marily herself contributed to the resistance as a courier. She used to cycle round her home district with transcripts of BBC news bulletins for distribution tucked into her knickers. This carried no little risk, since the German authorities had made it an offence punishable by death to listen to BBC broadcasts, or to make or distribute summaries.

Reprisals for attacks on the occupying forces were even more severe. The tariff for one German soldier killed was a hundred civilians taken at random and shot. A serious guerrilla attack could result in the burning of an entire village and the execution of its male population.

It never occurred to me that I might one day learn all this from first-hand accounts. We got on with our war in other parts of the Mediterranean. We fought alongside the Free French and Poles, but saw no Greeks until the autumn of 1944. Then, south of Rimini, we became aware of a new formation, with British uniforms and equipment and alert South European faces, and a few days later the Greek Brigade, formed and trained in Egypt, became the spearhead of the assault which drove the German army from Rimini and opened the Lombardy plain to the Allied advance. 1941 was in some measure avenged.

We lost sight of the Rimini Brigade (as it came to be called), but events shortly took a turn which brought Greece and me on to a collision course. In the last week of November 1944, the division (4th British) to which our regiment belonged was withdrawn from the front line after eight months of almost continuous action. The guns had to be cleaned and greased and left behind at Pescara, on the Adriatic coast, while we took the long road to Taranto, in the instep of Italy, there to await transport to Palestine and a period of rest. Taranto was depressing. It was hard to believe, looking at the flat drab landscape and the Moorish style of so many buildings (a legacy perhaps of Saracen occupation), that ancient Taras had been one of the richest and most important cities of the Greek civilisation in southern Italy and Sicily. The people were much less friendly than we had found them to be north of Rome, and some of them paraded their political maturity by daubing walls with helpful slogans such as 'Death to the Anglo-Saxon assassins!' On top of this, we in the Royal Artillery, while happy not to be living in holes in the ground for the time being, much disliked having been deprived of our 25-pounders. A Gunner regiment has no colours but its guns. They are the wellspring of its *esprit de corps*, and a battery without guns is like a hermit crab between shells.

These doldrums were not to last long. Across the Ionian Sea disturbing things were happening. During October the Germans had withdrawn their troops from Greece, more as part of their general retreat on all fronts than as a result of Allied or guerrilla pressure. A British parachute brigade entered the country to speed their withdrawal, and with the consent of the Greek government headed by George Papandreou, British 3rd Corps under General Ronald Scobie established its headquarters in the centre of Athens. Units of 46th and 4th Indian Divisions were dispersed throughout Athens and the rest of Greece, to assist with administration and as a check on ELAS's activities.

Almost at once the tensions and antagonisms of Greek politics, which had been suppressed or masked, first by the Metaxas regime and then by the German occupation, came into the open. These were many and various, but the most obvious was the struggle between Communists and non-Communists for control of the country. The Communist Party of Greece (KKE) had in ELAS a private military force at its disposal. The government army was generally anti-Communist and contained some strongly right-wing elements. During November the risk of an outbreak of violence grew ever greater. On Sunday 3 December shooting broke out at a demonstration in Constitution Square, and a number of people were killed. The leaders of ELAS accused the army and police of instigating bloodshed, and began a determined and well-organised attempt to take over Athens by force of arms. For better or worse, the British troops in the city were ordered to resist the attempt. Within a week the British army controlled the central area including Constitution Square, Mount Lycabettus and the Acropolis but not the adjoining hills; the Greek Army barracks at Goudi, at the foot of Mount Hymettus; part of the Piraeus, but not enough to allow use of the port by Allied shipping; and Hasani aerodrome. (This last is still the airport of Athens. The name Hasani, with its charming suggestion of flying carpets, was changed to Ellinikon at about the same time that Turkish coffee became Greek coffee.) Communication by road between these enclaves was kept open with difficulty and, especially in daylight, was hazardous. The rest of Athens was controlled by ELAS, which had brought in from the country districts a considerable number of men and weapons to augment its Athenian Corps of over 10,000. British Corps headquarters and the Greek government established in the Grande Bretagne Hotel in Constitution Square were both in the front line and threatened with attack. Reinforcements were urgently needed. As the nearest available uncommitted troops, that meant us.

The decision to commit British soldiers to the defence of Athens against ELAS was widely and sharply criticised at the time in the British Parliament and press, as well as in the United States and elsewhere. None of us was enthusiastic about shooting at men who had been our allies for three years, and whose tough endurance in the mountains, in the face of constant danger, many of our own compatriots had shared. The Army Bureau of Current Affairs felt it necessary to supply us with copious literature, which did its best to explain the intricate Greek scenario and to justify the British intervention. They were, I believe, preaching to the converted. Whatever the rights and wrongs of the original involvement, the present actuality was that we had comrades in arms who were in danger and needed us to rescue them.

The Bureau also provided helpful hints to guide our footsteps in Greek society. We were warned that nubile girls were invariably chaperoned by dragonish mammas, and that he who overcame that obstacle and robbed a Grecian maiden of her virginity might well get a brother's knife between his ribs, in the name of family honour. These challenges were, of course, accepted by the British Army with alacrity.

There was no time to be lost. A high proportion of the regiment was converted from artillery to infantry and flown in the bomb-bays of Liberator aircraft to Hasani, where they landed within range of ELAS small-arms fire. It was as close a shave as that. It was perhaps as well that the besiegers of the aerodrome did not know how long it had been since most of our gunners had looked along the sights of their rifles. Much of the divisional equipment had to be landed from assault craft on the bathing beaches of Faliron, between Hasani and the Piraeus, where a bridgehead was established as a base for an attack northwards into the city. Meanwhile, our number ones – the sergeants of the guns – sped back to Pescara with their gun-layers, to collect the darlings they had cosseted for so many years and had been obliged to abandon to the care of others unfamiliar with their quirks and necessities.

Somewhat to my relief, I was not required to play the part of an infantry officer, which I had been at pains to avoid by choosing the Gunners as my arm at the beginning of the war. The adjutant, I think it was, got it into his head that because I had had a classical education my knowledge of ancient Greek might make me useful at regimental headquarters and persuaded the CO that I should be temporarily detached from my battery as an assistant to himself. So it was that I came to Hellas, the mother of demi-gods and heroes, with a cargo of 25-pounders, tractors and ammunition trailers, in an American built Liberty ship named the *Sam Faithfull*.

The Liberty ship, a sort of freighter without frills, was a valuable contribution to the Allied war effort at a time when German submarines were sinking large quantities of merchant shipping. They were said to be built in the same number of days as a British yard would have lost in demarcation disputes, and the result was useful rather than pretty. The *Sam Faithfull* felt more like a boat-shaped steel box than a real ship and had a habit of shuddering from stem to stern, as if with an ague. Her officers said that the speed of our small convoy did not suit her, but maybe she was sulky at her lack of teak and brass.

We had genuine halcyon weather. South of Cape Matapan the sea was calm enough for kingfishers to nest on. Entering the Aegean we could see to starboard the western peaks of Crete. There some of the most dashing and romantic exploits of the resistance had been carried out, culminating in the kidnapping of the German commander on the island, General Kreipe; and there now, with a dogged impudence to match, the German garrison, stranded by the withdrawal which they had been unable to join, still held out – and were to do so for another five months.

We came into the Saronic Gulf by night, and my first view of Athens was at dawn, from a deck raked by a mean, thin wind from somewhere beyond the Black Sea. It was an unpromising landfall. The sky was completely covered by low flat cloud like a lead-coloured duvet, which eliminated both contrast and colour from the landscape. The Castello hill, behind the Piraeus, blocked the view of the heights and monuments of central Athens. The rest of the sprawling city, oddly featureless without the spires and towers of Western Europe and the domes and minarets of the Near East, made a huge dirty white lake with its edges lapping the feet of Mounts Hymettus and Parnes. The hills themselves seemed without charm or feature, bare as slagheaps.

The *Sam Faithfull* was anchored some way from the land, between the port and the island of Salamis, where once the Athenians destroyed the fleet of the Great King of the Medes and Persians. A dozen or so other ships, including two Swedish vessels carrying Red Cross workers and supplies, lay round us. The ELAS forces were still close enough to the quays to prevent any ships from entering port and discharging. A four-gun troop of 25-pounders, of 4th Indian Division, was in action on a small island near us. The thud and crack of mortars and the rattle of small-arms fire could be heard from the city. Under the cloud canopy two fighter planes buzzed back and forth like frustrated bluebottles.

Around midday word came that the infantry had cleared more of the port and that it was safe to go ashore. The *Sam Faithfull* crept through the harbour mouth and tied up at a quay. There followed a period of negotiation with the ship's crew, who, with a proper sense of priorities, demanded extra pay for unloading our equipment by means of the davits (there being, of course, no dockers to hand). Eventually the work began, a road convoy of vehicles and guns was assembled, and we set off along the coast road to Faliron. The streets were still and empty and smelt of nothing to suggest human activity.

In spite of Athens's chilly welcome, I was not depressed. Things could only get better, for it was evident that the tide of battle was turning against ELAS, and the sun was bound to come out sooner or later. Anticipation tingled inside me. For years the achievements of the Athenians had been my daily study, and now, when I least expected it, Fate masquerading as an outrageous fluke – or maybe it was the other way round – had deposited me to see for myself where it had all happened. The spice of my introduction to Greece lay in its sudden and unconventional nature. Everyone who has read ancient Greek feels, I suppose, a small special pleasure at finding that the street signs are written in the same familiar script and realising that he or she is walking along Hermes or Aristotle Street. (In Ithaca once, Marily and I lodged in a house at the junction of Odysseus and Eumaeus Streets, as if Homer's characters were a couple of local nineteenth-century worthies.) On the road to Faliron, this recognition struck home oddly and vividly. In his history of the war between Athens and Sparta which tore Greece apart and ended Athenian supremacy, Thucydides describes the class struggle between oligarchs and democrats (between Right and Left, as we might say) and in a celebrated passage recalls the brutal violence which it led to in Corcyra – modern Corfu. The word he uses for this state of civil strife is *stasis*. As our convoy moved along the coast, I noticed, at intervals by the roadside, boards on poles bearing that same word. The pages of Thucydides rose from my memory, and I had a crazy vision of the municipality of Athens keeping a stock of such boards for display whenever a revolution was in progress. Within a few moments I came to my senses and grasped that *stasis* indicates a bus-stop, but during that blink of time two millennia had been telescoped and the essential continuity of the Greek world brought home to me.

We spent two nights at Faliron and were then ready to go into action. It was Christmas Eve.

Two

The Faliron bridgehead had by now been enlarged and we established ourselves some way inland at Nea Smyrni, to the right of Syngrou Avenue, as you look towards the city. The district, as the name New Smyrna implies, was originally settled by refugees from Asia Minor, after the military debacle and the burning of Smyrna by the Turks in 1923. It had become a prosperous enough looking suburb – a little untidy at the edges where the war and the occupation had interrupted expansion and left half-finished building sites and streets. The houses were mostly unpretentious villas standing in small gardens.

It was odd, after the open country of Africa and Italy, to carry on the activities of a gun area in an urban setting, with householders trying to live their ordinary lives all round us. To everybody's relief, the immediate sense was that we had fallen among friends. As soon as we began to reconnoitre for a regimental HQ, a local man, Lefteri Frantzis, materialised like an amiable middle-aged genie and in fluent, richly accented English asked if he could help us. On learning that we needed, if possible, accommodation for an office, a cookhouse, the survey, signals and medical sections, an officers' mess and billets for up to a hundred men, he at once rounded up his neighbours and, with no apparent difficulty, persuaded them to give up whatever rooms we wanted. He and his wife housed the MO and his staff. For the mess we acquired a large opulent house with a caretaker, whose wife, Maria, undertook to cook for us, although she was so far pregnant that she could scarcely get near enough to the stove to do so.

104th Battery, whose guns were the first in action, found a

similar welcome and enjoyed a rewarding symbiosis with their neighbours, who gave the gunners beds and shelter, and got in return a share of rations and lighting. It was, for all the goodwill, neither a peaceful nor comfortable Christmas. There was no electricity in the area. Food was extremely short for the civilian population and the army was living on fourteen-day packs of hard rations, more nutritious than Lucullan. It was also, for the Nea Smyrniots, hellishly noisy. Few things are more alarming than a 25-pounder firing without warning nearby, particularly if you are in front of it. The blast also tended to break windows. After this had happened once or twice, a large handbell was installed at the command post, and this was rung as a warning that the guns were about to open fire.

Some of the fiercest fighting of the battle took place on Christmas and the following days, when ELAS made a determined attempt to stem the British advance from the coast. They also very nearly succeeded in blowing up the Grande Bretagne Hotel, with dynamite brought through the sewers from Omonia Square and placed directly beneath the building. But for the vigilance of a sentry named Bateman, who spotted some suspicious wires and raised the alarm, a fair number of generals and politicians would have been blown sky-high. Worse still, the gaiety of nations might have been dimmed by the loss of Osbert Lancaster, who was in the hotel at the time.

The battery's observation post was set up, appropriately, in the Athens Observatory, on a hill beside the Acropolis. An upper room there had a magnificent view of the north half of the city. On Boxing Day a convoy of armoured vehicles drew up outside the observatory and from a lorry emerged a portly man in an air commodore's uniform, who turned out to be Winston Churchill. (The Prime Minister, along with Anthony Eden and Field-Marshal Alexander, visited Athens at Christmas 1944 in an attempt to arrange a cease-fire.) Reverently saluted by the Field-Marshal and other top brass, the old man came into the observatory, climbed to the upper room, took a cigar from his attendant cigar-carrier, and lit it. He then, in total disregard of OP safety rules, advanced to the open window, blew a cloud of smoke over northern Athens and demanded to know where was the enemy. This brief encounter between the director of the British war effort and 104th Field Battery RA is not much publicised in the official records, and in fact represented the achievement of Mr Churchill's unquenchable ambition – usually thwarted by his prudent advisers – to visit the front of battle and to be within earshot of (in his own phrase) the 'martial sound of musketry'.

Perhaps he had hoped to see formations of ELAS marching in red coats. He seemed a trifle irritated to see nothing except houses and streets and to be told that the enemy could not be pointed out, as they were anywhere and everywhere. Urban guerrillas in civilian clothes make elusive targets. The use of artillery in central Athens was further restricted by a prohibition on shooting within a thousand yards of any ancient monument – a precaution which would have been appreciated by the citizens of Dresden and Coventry. (For that matter, if the Turks had not used the Parthenon as a powder magazine, nor the Venetians bombarded it with cannonballs, the temple would not be in its ruined state.)

In the event, we engaged targets further afield, and lobbed a number of shells in the general direction of my, as yet, undreamt-of life's companion, in one of the northern suburbs. She was not in serious danger from them. She had been warned that, because she had interpreted for the British Army after the liberation, she was on an ELAS black list and might be taken as a hostage. She had therefore been given refuge in the basement of a friendly consulate, and from there was smuggled in an ambulance to central Athens.

Down at Nea Smyrni we could see both sides of the factional coin. The fanatics of both right and left were infected with scribbler's itch, and their slogans screamed at each other from every available blank space of wall – 'Long live the King, He is coming, Death to the King, Long Live ELAS, Down with ELAS, EAM, EDES, KKE . . . ' We had direct experience of how civil war can affect a family. The house, across the street from Mr Frantzis's, part of which became the regimental office, belonged to a couple with two children, a son and a daughter. The boy had left home to join ELAS. A couple of days before we appeared on the scene soldiers of the Greek Army had come to the house and arrested the father for alleged involvement with ELAS. Since then his wife and daughter (a pretty girl of seventeen, called Marina, whom I had first seen at Mr Frantzis's conference) had had no word of him, nor had they any idea where he was being held. They were naturally very worried and insisted to us that the father had no personal connection with, nor even sympathy for, ELAS. In their opinion some spiteful neighbour had informed on the family, for no other reason than that the son of the house was a member of the Communist-led resistance.

Ted Howard-Vyse, the CO, took the view that, whatever the rights and wrongs of the arrest, it was quite improper for the army authorities to be holding a private citizen incommunicado at an undisclosed whereabouts. He detailed me to take Marina round the various Greek Army headquarters, and to help her to try to trace her father. We spent the better part of two days on this exercise, and eventually, with considerable difficulty, extracted the information that he had been removed to Egypt, where a military base was still maintained. It was a tiresome and frustrating inquiry, but made bearable by the fact that Marina was not only good-looking but also good-hearted, serious and affectionate, so that we passed the time agreeably together. First impressions of young Greek womanhood – not to mention the complete absence of the threatened chaperonage – were encouraging.

The reader may be suspecting, not unreasonably, that my

duties as temporary, acting, assistant adjutant were less than exacting. My usefulness as an interpreter had been seriously over-estimated. I could tell, from the sign above the door, whether a shop was a general store or a restaurant serving both beer and wine, but when a Greek opened his mouth I was unable to understand a word that he said. This was due in part to the dfference between the ancient and modern languages, which, although far less marked than the shift from, say, Latin to Italian or from Anglo-Saxon to modern English, is such that classical Greek has to be taught in Greek schools as a foreign tongue. Equally serious was the extraordinary way in which these people, not having been to British schools and universities, insisted on pronouncing their own language. Their vowels, in particular, had gone to pot to such an extent that I doubt if I would have recognised what language they were talking had I not known where I was.

In any case, we had very little need for an interpreter in Athens, where a high proportion of people spoke remarkably good English. In emergency we could call on Mr Frantzis for help and a good liaison grew up between him and me. The first Greek that I ever spoke to, he became the one I knew best during my early days in the country. He was a lean, sallow, eager man, balding and bespectacled, with a vaguely Armenian cast of countenance and a sudden alarming smile gleaming with gold teeth. His wife was a rather plain, self-effacing woman, dedicated to the house which was her pride. (The innermost shrine was a *saloni* with a parquet floor of such magnificence that it might only be trodden in slippers, like a mosque.) They had no children, but employed a hand-maid named Artemis, who looked about ten but must, I suppose, have been thirteen or fourteen. The house rang to the constant cries of 'Artemis' – 'At your service, madam'. The girl came from a poor family on one of the Aegean islands. It was still not uncommon at the time for such children to be put into domestic service, to relieve their family finances.

Mr Frantzis warmly admired England and Winston Churchill. I asked him what he did for a living in peacetime and he told me that he was a representative for 'Ko-Ats'. This had Aristophanic overtones, but I thought it improbable that he dealt in frogs' legs, and I looked blank. Mr Frantzis showed mild impatience. 'Ko-Ats,' he repeated, 'you know, Mr Macvicar – spool-threads.' I was relieved to find myself on home ground. 'Ko-Ats' was none other than the good old Scottish firm of J. & P. Coats, whose cotton reels of every hue and quality were to be found in all respectable workbaskets. In the piping times before the war, he had disseminated miles of spool-threads throughout Greece, and he hinted, with a golden leer, that he had been known as a breaker of hearts from Macedonia to Crete, like a latter-day Casanova among the seamstresses of Cassiopi.

Just before the end of the year, Mr Frantzis approached me diffidently. He and his wife were intending, he said, to see in the New Year with a small party at their house, to which they were inviting the medical orderlies who lodged with them and a couple of NCOs. He felt that in the interests of democracy – which, as he pointed out, our common struggle was all about – *all* ranks, including officers, should be represented at this international celebration. Would it, he wondered, be in order for him to invite the MO and myself? I admired both his impeccable sentiments and his delicate appreciation of the social niceties of army life. I assured him that there were no rules governing the composition of a Greek Hogmanay party in the middle of a battle, and that the doctor and I would be honoured to accept the invitation.

The company also included Mr Frantzis's brother-in-law and his wife, Mr and Mrs Palamas, so we were about a dozen in all. In spite of the tightness of supplies, there was a surprisingly large amount of Mavrodaphne and Samos wines and Mrs Frantzis had baked an enormous round *vasilopita* – the traditional New Year brioche which takes its name from Saint Basil (the first of January being his feast-day). A single gold coin was embedded in the cake and at midnight the whole of it was cut in segments, one for each of us present, one for the house and one 'for the stranger', who might be an angel in disguise. I forget now who got the piece containing the coin, and with it the luck of the coming year, but I do remember a lot of singing, including the usual garbled version of 'Auld Lang Syne' and a rousing rendering of 'Tipperary', which, as every foreigner knows, is seldom off the lips of the British Tommy. Some time in the small hours, Mr Palamas, a small unobtrusive man who had scarcely said a word all night, began to sing Spanish love-songs in a pure high tenor and sent us off to bed with a memory of heart-rending beauty.

For full dramatic effect the scene should have been played to an accompaniment of stuttering gunfire, but there was a lull in the fighting. The southern half of Athens had been cleared and our forces were preparing for the next drive to the north. On the morning after the party the colonel suggested that he and I might make our first visit to the Acropolis. We took his jeep and drove up Syngrou, free now from the hazard of snipers' bullets, into the heart of the city and up the slope of the road past the theatre of Dionysus, along which a million tourists now pass every year. Then it was empty. At the foot of the Acropolis, not a guide or photographer or stall. We left the jeep and walked up the path to the entrance, which was open and unmanned, and so on to the worn steps of the Propylaia. At the top, in front of us, stood the Parthenon.

I had not known quite what to expect. One forgets now that forty years ago there was almost no colour photography. I do not think that I had ever seen a picture of the temple except in black and white. I certainly remember one such photograph, in a school classroom, in which it resembled one of the neo-classical art galleries below the Mound in Edinburgh, blackened by years of steam engines and reeking lums. Nothing had prepared me for this apparition, honey-

31

golden against a forget-me-not winter sky. It looked to me weightless, as if it might float away to Olympus.

Ted Howard-Vyse and I were the only people on the rock. Sporadic rifle-shots spat out far below, and an occasional mortar bomb curved overhead. We reckoned that we might be inviting targets on the north side of the hill, so we gave the Erechtheion a miss, turned right past the little shrine of the Wingless Victory and skirted the sunlit south columns of the Parthenon, towards the museum. The day was cloudless. In the pellucid Athenian air of those days the city stretched sharp and clear to the shining sea.

The museum, like the Acropolis, was open and un-guarded. The colonel and I went inside, where we found chaos. The building had obviously been occupied as a com-mand post by the troops defending the rock. A grave stele of the fifth century B.C., delicately engraved with the graceful figure of a loved daughter, was lying where it had been set to serve as a writing table, its marble spattered with candle grease and ink. Presumably to give a better field of fire in case of attack, all the contents of the glass showcases had been removed and were lying on the floor in heaps.

The CO and I contemplated the mess with dismay. Our first reaction was to worry about the safety of the antiquities. The outcome of the battle for Athens was still undecided and there was no saying who might be the next visitors to the Acropolis. With little hesitation, I resolved to take something away for safe-keeping. I picked from one of the piles, more or less at random, two small bits of pottery – a female head broken from a votive statuette, and an undecorated dish about the size of a coffee saucer. Neither was particularly beautiful nor, so far as I could judge, of much value. The colonel took nothing, but did not lecture me on looting. I put the two objects in my pocket and we went back to the jeep.

I can only record that I did not think of myself as a looter. Ted Howard-Vyse and I were, I suppose, middling honest, yet whatever qualms we may have had we had little difficulty in stifling. The circumstances were undoubtedly special. Nevertheless I wonder if the purity of our motives was a complete excuse, or if mine, at least, were not mixed. Perhaps the incident says something about the fragile plant we call conscience and what war can do to it. It made me less ready than Byron was to be rude about Lord Elgin and the Marbles.

The story had a satisfactory ending. I kept, and got much pleasure from, my acquisitions for six months or so, shying away from any decision about their ultimate disposal. Wherever I was billeted they used to sit where I could see them in my bedroom, usually beside my hairbrushes. In the summer I was staying outside Athens, at Kifissia, in the house of an old lady whose nephew was an archaeologist. His wife had also come to stay there with her two young children, to avoid the heat of the city, and one day she noticed the little head and the dish. She asked me where I had got them, and I told her. 'You must give them back, you know,' she said, and with some relief I agreed. So, through her husband and without any fuss, they went back whence they had come. It had been a loan all along. It would be nice to think that the same principle will some day be accepted as applying to Lord Elgin's Marbles.

Two days later, the offensive to clear ELAS from the north half of Athens began and on 8 January we were able to leave Nea Smyrni and move the guns forward through the city to the northern suburb of Psychiko. Gun positions were prepared, but turned out to be unnecessary. We had – though we were not to know this – fired our last hostile rounds of the whole war. Psychiko, however, provided ample and comfortable quarters, the local residents were welcoming and we settled down pleasantly.

We had one last duty in Greece of a purely military nature. A cease-fire came into force on 14 January 1945 and one term of the agreement was that ELAS should surrender their arms.

33

There was a strong concentration of ELAS soldiers in Boeotia, from where the incursion into Attica and Athens had been launched. At the end of the month the regiment was sent there, as a precaution against trouble when the arms were due to be handed over. By this time I had rejoined my old comrades in 112/117th Field Battery, which was stationed at Livadhia.

Livadhia is a fair-sized town in western Boeotia, on what used to be the main road from Athens to the north, before the National Highway was built. From it the road to Delphi starts its slow climb up the flank of Parnassus and in the old days of much slower road travel it was a favourite spot at which to refresh oneself with souvlakia and yaourti. Now it lay silent, dominated by sullen cliffs, muffled by a foot of snow and fragrant with the wood smoke which rose from every chimney. It was the only place in Greece where I have not felt at ease. The language problem restricted communication, but this was unimportant compared with the constraint that we felt between us and the townsfolk. Livadhia had been an ELAS centre and it was plain that the inhabitants were either pro-ELAS (and thus, *ipso facto,* anti-British Army) or else were too afraid of reprisals to display their real feelings. On the day of the arms surrender the warriors of the Resistance marched into town, magnificent in their beards, moustaches and crossed bandoliers, their leaders before them on horseback. A heterogeneous collection of muskets and fowling-pieces were ritually laid down without a friendly word or smile and the men of the Left departed to prepare themselves for the next round of the struggle. It was a melancholy contrast to the exhilaration of the first comradeship of 1940.

So ended our strange looking-glass campaign. We went back to Athens, and began our existence as an army of friendly occupation.

Three

'There's one really super girl called Màrrily Vulgàris,' Ted Brown said in the officers' mess. In this manner, with an unsolicited testimonial and a subtle mispronunciation of her names, which made her sound like a not very special wild flower, my life's partner first came to my attention.

The reason why Ted was bandying a lady's name about the mess was that he had spent the day recruiting assistants to serve behind the counters of the Officers' Shop in the centre of Athens. This institution, like the NAAFI and an officers' club, had been set up very soon after the British forces entered Greece in October 1944. Everyone of whatever rank was almost bound to pass through Athens, at some time or another. The troubles of the winter closed down all these ancillary services and dispersed the locally engaged staff. As soon as peace returned to the city, it fell to the lot of Lieutenant Brown, who had pre-war experience of retail haberdashery, to get the shop working again. Time was short. Brigadiers and junior subalterns alike were running out of socks and underwear. The resourceful Ted went round the houses of Psychiko in which the regiment was quartered and asked the parents of any likely girl if they would spare her to act as a saleslady until long-term employees were found. So Marily could be seen in working hours at the issue bay, where we collected our new berets and button-sticks.

When at last I met her, I saw a pale girl of eighteen, with very dark hair, a direct intelligent regard and a pretty mouth which turned up comically at the corners when she smiled. I thought she was nice and amusing, but not heart-stopping. The assessment was mutual. Neither of us imagined for a moment that we would one day be husband and wife.

However, I got to know her fairly well, along with some of her close friends – her *parea*, as the Greeks say – who lived in the same neighbourhood. They were a group of girls most of whom had been at school together during the German occupation, which had closed many of the places of entertainment and – because of the shortage of petrol – made travel, even into Athens, extremely limited. The friends had been thrown back on their own resources and had used them well. They had a good knowledge of European literature, discussed political, social and philosophical issues, and all spoke English, and often another foreign language. (Marily in particular, although she had never been outside Greece, spoke almost faultless English, with only a trace of an accent.) Each of them – Daisy, Deppie, Yolanda, Kakia and the others – was a very distinct individual, but collectively they made on me an impression of freshness, good sense and capacity for affection, which reminded me of Homer's Nausicaa. This romantic literary association was, I daresay, encouraged by the fact that the exigencies of war had prevented me from having an intelligent conversation with an amusing woman for over a year.

Female society of this kind was an unexpected bonus in our lives and confirmed the expectations that Marina had aroused in me. But the pleasure which, from the very first, I experienced at being in Greece did not depend only on its girls. It was the lifting of a weight. In North Africa, the French, with a few memorable exceptions, had supported Pétain rather than de Gaulle and did not forgive us for the raid on the naval base at Oran, which destroyed a large portion of their fleet. (The indigenous Kabyles disliked us almost as strongly as they did the French and used to amuse themselves by rolling boulders down hillsides on to army road convoys.) The Egyptians regarded us with resigned and understandable loathing. The Italians had welcomed us warmly enough, as deliverers from German depredations – and had protected and fed many escaped Allied prisoners of war – but it was hard to feel completely at one with a nation that had changed sides in the middle of the war. Now, for the first time in two years, I felt at home.

It was self-evident that certain Greeks did not care for us, bitterly resented our thwarting of their political ambitions, and would have thrown us out of their country if they could. If I ever met any, they were not foolish enough to reveal their thoughts. The citizens of Psychiko, among whom we moved, made no secret of their relief that they had not had to exchange a German occupation for a Communist revolution. But, even when allowance was made for an immediate reaction of gratitude, it was good to be with men and women who had stood together with us, without wavering, in the common cause. We could shake hands and look each other in the eye as partners in adversity and triumph. I was surprised and rather moved, to discover that the partnership was seen by many Greeks as much more long-standing. We basked, in fact, in the reflected glory of Lord Byron.

Byron was inspired by the ideal of liberty and the glories of ancient Greece. He did not much care for the freedom-fighters whom he financed and tried to organise. He found them quarrelsome, vainglorious, unreliable and the most frightful liars. His death, after only three months in the country, may have come in time to spare him fatal disillu-sionment. But it made him, for the Greeks, a hero and a martyr for their cause. The fact that a rich and famous nobleman could devote both his fortune and his person to the revolt against the Turks, and share the hardships of the field even to sickness and death, left an indelible impression on the Greek consciousness. William Wheeler, who had been a pri-vate in the 51st Light Infantry Regiment at the Battle of Waterloo, was an army schoolmaster in Corfu in April 1824, when Byron died at Missolonghi. In one of his letters home, Wheeler tells how on 20 May the brig carrying Byron's body to England put in at Corfu. He met a Greek acquaintance in town and told him that Lord Byron was leaving Greece for the last time. 'He replied, ' says Wheeler, '"No never," then striking his left breast at the same moment his soul rushed into his eyes, "He will always live here and in the hearts of my countrymen."'

So it has proved. Streets are named after him and memorial busts and inscriptions stand, in towns and villages all over Greece, Greeks often mentioned him affectionately in conversation with me. They were on the whole tactfully silent on the subject of my other fellow Scot Lord Elgin and his notorious Marbles.

Noble sentiments apart, I liked the Greeks. I enjoyed the lively intelligence and quickness in the uptake; the self-mocking (and sometimes Aristophanically dirty) humour; the readiness to turn any occasion into a party; the ungrudging hospitality. One Athenian I knew told me that he had remonstrated with a friend for the extravagance of the entertainment that he was offering night after night to British troops. The friend had replied that he was so pleased to see the English that he did not care if he went bankrupt. Along with the hospitality, which was conspicuous in every class of society, went a personal interest in the details of one's age, occupation and family. There is an element of tradition and convention in this catechism, and in the hospitality itself, but they never seemed anything but genuine. Nowhere have I felt more strongly that I talked to people man to man, across all differences of background, culture or class. Robert Burns would have approved.

One had to admire, if not always to applaud, Greek commercial initiative. Within days of the end of hostilities street traders were doing brisk business in stocks of Red Cross provisions – landed, apparently, from the Swedish ships we had seen lying off the Piraeus before Christmas. Mr Frantzis himself was a sturdy example of the species *homo mercantilis*. I continued to see him regularly. We were anxious to start a small regimental club, and he busied himself in finding premises for this in a taverna in the Plaka district.* He clearly hoped to make himself indispensable to our regiment, and if possible to the entire British army in Athens, and I have no doubt that he cultivated my acquaintance to that end. I did not hold it against him. The man had to live, and there was small prospect of the Coats agency reviving in the immediate future. Besides, he had an endearing eagerness which made me laugh. He had a passionate interest in the rapidly rising value of the gold pound (not surprisingly, I thought, with so much precious metal in his mouth) and whenever I met him he would greet me breathlessly with the latest information on the subject.

He took me to see the spool-thread headquarters, which turned out to be a very small room in an office block in Aeolus Street. (Celestially named, this is in reality a dingy commercial canyon, redeemed only by the startling view of the Acropolis which floats beyond its end.) It contained an elderly desk, two plain wooden chairs and shelf upon shelf of reels of cotton, in all the colours of the spectrum, waiting to bring polychromatic activity to the sewing machines of the Aegean. Mr Frantzis did not seem depressed. Buoyant with visions of his incipient career as a military purveyor, he took me out to lunch at the Papahimonas (Father Christmas) taverna. It had no heating and felt like the North Pole. One wall was lined with enormous wine barrels and we drank potent, brusque retsina from one of them until the temperature did not matter. This was the first time that I tasted retsina in draught, as ideally it ought to be drunk – and has been drunk since first the natives of Attica started doctoring their casks with pine resin. Michael Akominatos, the metro-

* This became known as the 43 Club, after the numerals displayed on the regiment's vehicles. Mr Frantzis supplied most of its local liquor. The walls of the taverna were decorated with a lively mural, depicting scenes of Anglo-Greek friendship and jollity. The artist was a young gunner, Paul Wyeth, who had the reputation of being the least cooperative soldier in his battery. War was an irrelevant intrusion on his art, and he once tried to escape from detention by swimming away into the Mediterra-néan. A marvellous painter, he later, in real life, had a well-deserved success in his career.

politan of Athens, writing to a friend around 1200 A.D., described the local wine as seeming 'to be pressed from the juice of the pine rather than from that of the grape', and my first impression of retsina was that of something more like turpentine than wine. However, not wanting to waste the bottle which I had ordered, I persevered. After the fourth glass it became delicious and addictive.

Athens came slowly back to life in the bright, cold days of January and February. To begin with there was almost no traffic in the streets except military cars and trucks. Then the trolley-bus service started to run and later a few ordinary buses. But petrol was still very short and there were practically no private cars on the roads. The city remained a quiet place, to an extent scarcely imaginable today. A few restaurants, such as Jimmy's, reopened quickly and before long the cafe habitués were back in their accustomed tables at Zonar's and Floca. Traditionalists left over from the Edwardian age emerged from hibernation and walked stiffly in sedate suits and hats to the old Vyzantion coffee-house, to while away the hours with backgammon and long pulls at the bubbling narghiles.

In the main, of course, one observed the city as an outsider. Our everyday world was that of the regiment and the battery. Routine duties, the maintenance of guns and vehicles, the provision of guards for various installations, and so on, occupied most of the daytime hours. Off duty, we were in each other's company in the mess more often than not and were self-sufficient in our amusements. The officers' club provided a reasonable meal, the bars of the Grande Bretagne and King George V hotels were civilised rendezvous for a drink, while for night life there was always, and only, the Argentina.

The Argentina, which had nothing Latin American about it except its name, had a bar, dance floor and band, and a cabaret. This last consisted of a number of turns of stunning mediocrity, designed to enhance the attractions of its star and *raison d'être,* La Bella Smara. She was a mature but well-preserved singer, with a powerful talent and dominating personality, who wrung every drop of emotion and drama from her songs. She had refused to sing for the occupying forces of Italy and Germany and was admired in Athens for her patriotism and financial sacrifice. She did not stint herself for us.

Between shows, La Bella Smara would install herself at a table bedside the dance floor, whence her magnificent eyes reconnoitred the room for a man to keep her company.

I was never more surprised. There I was, minding my own business at the bar with a couple of friends and a glass of three-star koniak, when a waiter sidled up to me and said that Kyria Smara wished me to join her at her table. I was (and, I think, looked) a rather innocent young man. I did not have, nor was I ambitious to have, any experience of southern European cabaret *chanteuses* of a certain age. I suggested to the waiter that he had got the wrong man, but he assured me that it was I and no one else that the lady wanted. Courtesy and curiosity impelled me to yield to this flattery. I strode with a nonchalant man-of-the-world bearing into the lime-light. A hidden bottle of champagne appeared, two glasses were filled, we drank to each other, the band struck up, I was gathered from my seat and we were on the floor together. What was the tune? Was it a quickstep, a slow foxtrot, or tango? I was too dazed to take it in. At that time I was a diffident and clumsy dancer, but controlled and en-gulfed by La Bella Smara's warm and supple body I was Fred Astaire. For once the poetry of motion was no cliché.

Back at the table embarrassment set in. I was not just out of my depth. I was out of my depth in full view of two hundred pairs of eyes. I drank another glass of sweetish bubbly, paid for the bottle, made my excuses and retired to the back benches. La Bella Smara did not try to stop me. I suspect I was not quite what she had been looking for. I never saw or heard of her again, but I have a soft spot for her yet for giving me something oddly special to remember.

The Argentina had not finished with me. As we were about to leave, I caught a girl's lively dark eye. She was quite young, sitting by the wall with a friend who looked even younger. She grinned at me – I guessed that she must have witnessed my brief hour of unsought fame. I spoke to her, and we exchanged some banter. I discovered that she lived at Psychiko, I gave her a lift home and we arranged to meet again. So began my involvement with Euterpe.

She was small and neat, moved quickly, laughed loudly, and grasped at pleasure with both hands. She was sharp but without intellectual pretensions, wore too much lipstick and could, as a party trick, whistle like a nightingale. From the outset she made no secret whatever of the fact that she fancied me. I had never met any girl remotely like her. I fell for her with a heavy thump.

Euterpe lived with her father and stepmother not far from our mess. He was a respectable, serious, middle-aged civil servant, with a quiet equally respectable second wife. Euterpe must, I think, have taken after her divorced mother, whom I never met. She had been at school with Marily, but was not one of her *parea*. She would not have been accepted. During the occupation she had been very friendly with a soldier in the German army, a young Austrian called Hans, and this had put her in the eyes of her schoolfellows beyond the pale. I did not know this, of course – at least not to begin with – but I understood from occasional remarks that she made that she had known and liked a German. It made no difference to the first flush of my feelings for Euterpe. So far as either of us knew, she might never see or hear from him again.

Two or three weeks after its return to Athens from Boeotia, the regiment was sent north again, this time to the small town of Stylis, on the gulf of Lamia. Our role was humanitarian. The German army had carried out some of their worst reprisals on the civilian population in both the mountains and the coastal strip, all up the east coast of Greece. The countryside had been stripped of supplies. Relief organisations such as the Red Cross and UNRRA were trying to deal with the immediate distress, and also give a fresh start to the damaged rural economy. For this they needed accurate information about local needs. Our task was to obtain this, village by village. Billeting in civilian houses was not possible, so we went under canvas in an olive grove, which is not a warm way to live in Greece in early March. We then prepared to carry out our survey.

Before this got under way I was back in Athens again. I was keen to see more of Euterpe and had no difficulty in getting a week's local leave. (I had only taken a total of about two weeks on leave in the same number of years since we had sailed for North Africa.) Mr and Mrs Frantzis had been kind enough to say that I might stay with them if I needed a bed in Athens, and I took advantage of the offer.

Mr Frantzis's business enterprises gave evidence of flourishing. The spool-thread sanctum tended to be seriously overcrowded, for its occupant had taken on as partners little Palamas, his brother-in-law, and a taciturn man named Papapetrakopoulos, who strongly resembled Mr Mikoyan of the Soviet Politburo. The small table carried an impressive stock of notepaper and invoices, all with the heading 'Frantzis Palamas and Papapetrakopoulos. General Merchants and Purveyors of Wines and Spirits to HM Forces.' Mr Palamas, from what I had seen of him, seemed an improbable member of the troika, and I said as much, privately, to Mr Frantzis. Mr Frantzis laughed and said, 'Ach, at business he is no good at all, but for a parrrty Palamas is magnificent.' Remembering the plaintive love songs which had been the little man's contribution to the last 'parrrty', I wondered what he meant. I was soon to find out.

It was Carnival time, just before the start of *Sarakosti*, the

43

Greek Lent. One evening, having had dinner in town, I came down to the house in Nea Smyrni at about ten o'clock. Mr Frantzis was in front of the bathroom mirror, blackening his face with burnt cork. He was, he explained, about to join his wife at a fancy dress party, disguised as an Egyptian food vendor. Once made up, he wrapped a sheet round himself, devised a head-dress from a towel, and equipped himself with a tin tray full of rice and nuts. His horn-rimmed glasses added an intellectual flavour to the transformation. He then suggested that I should also come to the party, where he assured me that I would be very welcome. I saw no good reason for refusing.

The pair of us set out and walked to a neighbour's house. There we found Mrs Frantzis, a dozen or so couples from nearby, and a large Greek army major of ponderous aspect. He and I were in uniform. The other men wore various home-contrived costumes, mostly of an Asiatic type, except Mr Palamas, who was in drag, giving an uncanny impersonation of a dowdy but flirtatious schoolmistress. The ladies – obviously by pre-arrangement – were his pupils, in short skirts, bobby-socks and pigtails tied with red bows. The evening took a little time to warm up. We sat drinking very sweet wine with strained politeness, till Mr Palamas could stand it no more. In his awful cloche hat, he climbed upon the major's lap and began to make amorous advances to him. The act was so convincing and so sustained that the officer showed increasing signs of embarrassment. I began to be afraid that he would lose patience and punch Palamas on the nose. However, his tormentor knew when to stop. The ice was broken and the company became infected with *kefi*, the spirit that is the vital ingredient of a Greek – or indeed any – party.

It transpired that our gathering was no more than a warm-up to the real entertainment of the night. This was happening up the road, at the Stamboulides' house. We debouched into the ill-lit street and, looking like a troupe of middle-aged mummers, walked the few hundred yards to the next stop. Here there were further supplies of food and drink and a gramophone was playing for dancing. Our host, who was short, stout and elderly, led the revelry. He was an expert in the Viennese waltz and whirled partner after partner round the room. All at once a hush fell, followed by a murmur, rising to a babble, of bad news. It was translated to me that the waltzing had been too much for Mr Stamboulides, who had suffered a heart attack. With spontaneous sympathy – combined, no doubt, with a reluctance not to be in at the death – all the guests rushed upstairs to the bedroom. The poor man was lying on a large double bed, blue in the face, gasping for breath and unconscious.

Mr Frantzis turned to me. Did I think it would be possible to get a British army doctor? I knew that there was, not far away, a still operational casualty clearing station of the 4th Indian Division and I agreed to try. Mr Frantzis and Mr Palamas insisted on coming with me and we set off up the hill. It was now well past midnight. We penetrated the RAMC building and eventually found four uniformed doctors, three British and one Indian, playing bridge.

They were a credit to their profession. The apparition in the small hours of a rather tight lieutenant, a white-robed oriental and a female impersonator they treated as completely normal. The senior officer listened to what I had to say and without hesitation said to the Indian doctor: 'You're dummy. You'd better go'. The unlucky man collected a small case and accompanied us to Mr Stamboulides' house. There, the whole cast were still in the bedroom. There was evidence that the old-fashioned remedy of cupping had been applied to the protagonist, who looked, if possible, even worse than before. The doctor asked some questions about his history, examined him, gave him an injection, and stood back. He was a very tall slender young man and he towered above the pashas, fakirs, Barbary pirates and elderly schoolgirls who crowded vociferously round him. He fended them off with

45

waves of his long brown hands and looked at me despairingly. 'What do they want?' he asked. I told him. 'They want to know if he will live.' 'I think not,' the doctor said, and departed into the night.

He was right, of course. About a quarter of an hour later, a mirror held to Mr Stamboulides' lips showed that he had stopped breathing. His body was at once stripped naked and covered with a sheet and his wife and two daughters knelt at the foot of the bed and began to wail, all together and without stopping. We did not try to stop them but let them cry out their pain until they were able to find relief in tears. I thought it time to go. Mr and Mrs Frantzis said that they would stay with the others for a while, so I left the ruins of the Carnival and went off to bed.

The funeral took place the very next afternoon. The Frantzises and I agreed that it would be fitting for me to attend – and indeed I felt that I had come to know Mr Stamboulides rather well. We walked back along the street to the house, where, in the centre of the large room round which he had spun twelve hours earlier, he lay calm and pale in an open coffin. We bowed respectfully over him. Then Mrs Frantzis joined the women, who were sitting round the room, and her husband and I went out into the garden. It was sunny, with a cold spring breeze. The male mourners, who included most of last night's party, stood about, smoking cigarettes. After a time, a hearse drawn by two black horses arrived. The coffin was placed aboard, and, led by the bearded priest in Orthodox chimney-pot hat, and a thurifer, the cortège proceeded on foot to the church.

The coffin was laid in the middle of the nave, with the dead man's face still exposed. The congregation stood round it in a semicircle. The *papas* intoned long prayers, interspersed with responses from a psaltis. Finally, one of the mourners, clearly a close friend of the family, stepped forward and delivered a funeral oration of such eloquence that everyone except myself (being unable to understand it) was reduced to tears.

46

Even the priest was obliged to retire behind the *iconostasis* to compose himself, dabbing his eyes with a large handkerchief which he produced from inside his vestments. We filed out past the dead man. Each of his friends kissed him on the forehead. I suppose I should have done too, but some sort of awkwardness held me back.

That evening I said goodbye to Euterpe and on the next day I drove back along the road north: through Eleusis of the Mysteries; over the hills to seven-gated Thebes, city of Cadmus and Oedipus; passed Livadhia and Chaeronea, where Philip of Macedon extinguished the liberties of Hellas; up the Valley of the Kephisus, in whose marshes the Frankish chivalry floundered and perished at the swords of the Catalan Company; over the twisting pot-holed hill road above Thermopylae; and so down into Phthiotis, homeland of Achilles and his Myrmidons. The hundred miles of the way were haunted by ghosts of myth and history and I was scarcely conscious of them. Greek flesh and blood had crowded them from my mind.

I was now about to see for the first time that side of Greece which stands over against Athens and the big towns, the world of the villages – to most philhellenes the 'real' Greece, though it is a matter for question how much longer it can survive in its traditional character. Our investigations into rural needs had to be carried out village by village of Achilles' old kingdom. Our camp in the olive grove was close to the sea, and from it we covered first the coast and then the hills behind. The sun grew daily stronger, and spring unrolled with amazing speed a carpet of flowers – white, pink and purple anemones, violet and yellow irises, and the branching candlesticks of the asphodel.

One or two villages were visited each day, in accordance with a prearranged programme. A jeep would carry an officer, two armed gunners (just in case of over-enthusiastic left-wing resentment) and an interpreter. My regular interpreter,

Pavlos, was a gentle and courteous middle-aged man who had retired and returned to his home after many years in the United States. He was thus one of the many Greeks sometimes known collectively as 'Brooklies', from the district of New York City where they formed a colony, or as 'Hello boys'. (They used to have a bad reputation among English travellers in Greece, who complained that America had converted them from decent respectful sons of the soil into boastful materialists bent on running down their own country. Fortunately, Pavlos had none of these unpleasant traits.) I was also armed with a large form, always referred to, for some bureaucratic reason, as a proforma, which set out comprehensively all types of supply for human wants.

Arriving at a village, we would be met by the *proedros* (village president) and a few of the senior villagers, including, if the place was big enough to possess them, the priest and schoolmaster. We then worked our way through the form, entering their estimates of what the village needed. Sometimes these were so large as to suggest either that all the inhabitants were starving and naked, or that they were taking the sensible precaution of asking for three times what they hoped to get. That however was UNRRA's concern, not ours.

At the end of formal business we all repaired to the *kafeneion*, where wine, ouzo or brandy was produced, and healths drunk with expressions of international goodwill. I do not remember ever leaving a village empty-handed. Always there was a small present, of a few eggs or some freshly caught fish. At Achilleion – could this have been the hero's actual birthplace or summer palace? – they had woven a wreath of laurel and insisted on placing it round my neck.

The villages along the coast, with their gardens and fields, had an air of potential prosperity. The first hill village I went to was different. We got the jeep to it with difficulty, up a mile of appalling track. It stood on a little bare plateau. No trace of cultivation was in sight. The small houses, dotted about as if at random, looked more like sheds than human habitations. Five lean, unsmiling men greeted us without warmth. Pavlos prepared to fill up the form. They wanted nothing. Food? – they had enough to eat; clothing? – as we could see, they were not short of it; medicines? – nobody in the village was ill. The interview ground to a halt, and we all fell silent. There was no suggestion of adjourning for an ouzo. I suspected that this was a Communist village – for there were such – which simply wished to have nothing to do with capitalist charity. I was about to say goodbye, when from over the brow of a hill appeared a couple of dozen children, all carrying huge armfuls of blue wild hyacinths. Urged on by their mothers, they shyly offered the flowers to us and began to pile the jeep with them. I was taken aback by the thought of driving back to camp bedecked with bluebells, and I suppose that I made demurring noises, for Pavlos said urgently: 'You must take them. They will be very hurt. You know, they have nothing else to offer you.'

A few days later I was sent on a course at the artillery school at Civitavecchia, north of Rome. I retraced my steps to Athens and from there took ship for Italy.

Four

During the three or four weeks that I was out of Greece, Orthodox Easter came and went, Hitler and Eva Braun descended into the Berlin bunker, never to be seen again, and the war in Europe ended, with the premature demise of the 1,000-year Reich. The battery returned to base in Psychiko, and a thoughtful friend arranged for me to be billeted with Euterpe and her family.

I had left Athens in the spring. Now it was summer – *kalokairi*, the fair season. Life spilled out on to terraces and balconies and the café tables in the squares and on the pavements. Girls were light and bright in cotton dresses, while we discarded battledress for khaki drill. Restaurants came out of winter quarters into their courtyards and gardens. The air was dry and invigorating, warm by day and cool at night. The light painted with a lyrical clarity of line and colour the columns and tumbled marbles of the ancient city, and the shabby, comfortable dignity of the nineteenth-century houses, with their faded stucco and neo-classical pilasters and balustrades.

I was seeing it all, of course, with the eye of a young man's fancy. Our military duties were not exacting and I had a lot of spare time, much of which I spent with Euterpe. She took my education in hand, telling me with truth that I should be ashamed of my poor modern Greek after nearly six months in the country. Since most of the Athenians I dealt with spoke good English, I had not troubled to progress beyond the 'Good morning-please-thank you' stage. Now, under intense instruction, I began to get my tongue round the unfamiliar sounds, to master the grammar (child's play compared with what I had gone through at school), and to put together sentences at a simple colloquial level. Once over the first hurdles, I found a knowledge of classical Greek a considerable help and was impressed by the extent to which this people were using the same language as their forefathers of two and a half millennia ago.

As the summer heat increased we swam a lot. With such a shortage of civilian transport, both public and private, the young ladies of Psychiko found the army very useful; and most afternoons saw mixed bathing parties set off by truck and lorry for Faliron, or further afield to the quiet pine-ringed coves of Kavouri and Vouliagmeni, then almost completely natural and unspoiled. We walked in the evening up the path through the small pine trees to the top of Lycabettus, which then had no funicular or restaurant, only the chapel and a tiny café. There, over an ouzo, or a spoonful of white *masticha* in a tumbler of cold water – known popularly as a submarine – one could watch the flat backcloth of Hymettus slide into relief, as the dropping sun threw its gullies into shadow and stained its flanks with deepening rose and purple. Then came the moment when the whole of Athens put on the violet crown of twilight and above the rock of the Acropolis the first lone star appeared, followed by another and another, faster and faster, till all the sky was hung with lamps as big as lemons and spanned by the Milky Way, like a bridge for angels and lovers.

The Athens Symphony Orchestra came to life and we went to hear Beethoven in the old theatre of Herodes Atticus, sitting in romantic discomfort among the rocks and prickly pears above the circles of stone seats, where bats flittered and squeaked round us in the dusk. Afterwards, as on so many nights, we ate out, and Euterpe broadened my education on the dance floor under the canopy of stars.

I did not have occasion to revisit the Acropolis, nor did I go out of my way to seek one. For all their power as a symbol, the rock and its monuments represented a culture which had no hold on the hearts of the Greek people. I came to understand more and more how strongly they still felt the pull of the long-vanished Byzantine Empire. The Great Idea – *I Megali Idhea* – the dream of a recaptured Constantinople as the centre of the Greek world, might be dead. Spiritual nostalgia for the city was not. Every child knew the legend that at the end of the last liturgy in the great Church of the Holy Wisdom the priest had taken up the sacred vessels and vanished with them into the wall of the sanctuary, out of which it is said that he will reappear when Ayia Sophia is restored to Christian worship. It is also said that Greek Orthodox priests wear black robes, and their hair unshorn, in mourning for the death of the city and its last emperor. It is a fact that because 29 May 1453, when the Ottoman Turks took the city of Constantine, was a Tuesday, no Greeks, if they can help it, will begin an enterprise of any moment on that day of the week.

Greeks have never struck me as conspicuously pious. Most of them, even forty years ago when their society was less secular and material than it is today, sat lightly to their religion. The Orthodox Church was respected for the lead it had always given in resistance to foreign oppression (the latest and finest example being the gigantic Archbishop Damaskinos, who held the Regency at the time of which I write), but the attitude towards individual priests tended to be one of amused tolerance. In Corfu they are supposed to bring bad luck. (The traditional method for a man to avert this, on meeting a priest, is to touch his trousers discreetly in the region of the private parts.) Nevertheless, the depth of the underlying Christian ethos, in its Greek Orthodox manifestation, was apparent from marks of tradition and habit – the general observance of major festivals and fasts, often with their special dishes; the celebration, with processions, feasting and dancing, of the annual *paniyiria* of local saints; the oil lamps which flickered in front of icons in many private houses and at wayside shrines; women in the city-bound bus crossing themselves as it passed a church.

I was beginning to fill in the expanse of ignorance between the Greece of my schooling and the Greece with which war had involved me and to get a view, dim at first, of Hellenism as an enduring spirit that had created the civilisation of the Mediterranean and handed it over to Rome, established Greek kingdoms in Central Asia and influenced the Buddhist art of the Indus valley, converted the eastern half of the Roman Empire into a Greek state which stood as the preserver of classical learning and the bastion of Christianity against Persians, Saracens and Turks, while Europe struggled through the Dark Ages, and finally kept its people's faith and pride fiercely alive under four hundred years of Ottoman oppression. Most remarkable of all, although the Greek lands had been overrun, infiltrated and settled by floods of Slavs, Albanians, Armenians and other Near Eastern peoples, the genius of Hellas had absorbed them all and turned them into something instantly and unmistakably recognisable as Greek, with essentially the same speech and the same good and bad qualities as the men and women in Homer's poems and the plays of the Athenian dramatists.

Such matters occupied little of my time, which was filled by more immediate concerns. In June I took command of a troop in 104th Battery, which was stationed at Philothei, a mile further out of Athens, and left Psychiko for the last time. I had more to do and also had to get to know a whole new set of men. It was a wrench to leave my good companions in 112/117, but 104 was an excellent battery, well commanded by Tony Babington, with whom I became very friendly.

The battery was unusual, at that time, in having six horses on its strength. In May, when Germany surrendered, the garrison in Crete felt that they could now honourably give themselves up. My fellow officer, Bill Hancock, who spoke good German, was among the interpreters sent from Athens to help in the hand-over. The colonel, who had a high peacetime reputation as a horseman, learned that there were German army horses to be disposed of and conceived the idea of starting a regimental saddle school. He got permission to acquire six horses for this purpose. Bill made the arrangements, and in due course the horses were delivered to RHQ, including a gentle little mare in foal. They were looked after by 104th Battery and supplied with feed by the army commissariat, which apparently saw nothing out of the way in a fully mechanised unit keeping horses. (Bill also took over from its handler, a German sergeant, a military Alsatian dog, which was trained to bring a man down and if required, to savage him. Rex regularly went swimming with us and when taken to a restaurant used to nip the waiters' ankles from a vantage-point under the table.)

There was a sense that the war against Japan would not last much longer and that we were in sight of a return to civilian life. Now that it was possible to cross Europe by land, home leave was getting under way on a large scale. Everyone, especially the married men, was becoming preoccupied with dates of leave and possible demobilisation. The military duties were boring and repetitive and it was hard to avoid becoming edgy and restive. Japan surrendered on 15 August and nothing much mattered after that.

By that time the regiment had moved still further north of Athens, to the rather smart, old-fashioned dormitory town of Kifissia. On high ground under Mount Pendeli, with its marble quarries, it was pleasantly cool and we all had good quarters in solid houses with tree-shaded gardens. I enjoyed a spacious bedroom, in the Villa Lily, which stood back from the main road through Kifissia. The house was named after its owner, Lily Calvocoressi, a strong-minded old lady with snow-white hair, who had defied orders and risked being shot when she sped the departing German troops on their way past the house by displaying an outsize Greek flag and calling 'Long live Greece' at them from her garden gate. The household also comprised her sister, Mrs Pandazidhou, and their nephew's wife, Lia Kalliga. They were good company and I was made at home.

I still visited Nea Smyrni occasionally, but I allowed my relationship with Mr Frantzis to cool. Marina told me that she had good reason to believe that it was he who had laid the information against her father which led to his arrest on suspicion of ELAS activity. I could not very well accuse Mr Frantzis of doing such a disservice to one of his nearest neighbours and there was no way of testing the truth of the matter. I simply stopped seeing him and, a little guiltily, ended the friendship which had given me such a vivid introduction to Athenian suburban society.

My affair with Euterpe was also losing its first idyllic charm. We had too little in common for a good permanent relationship – I daresay that in my heart I had always known this – and now that my days in Greece must soon be numbered, the question of the future for both of us became pressing. Also, the shadow of Hans showed a tendency to fall between us. Yet we were very fond of each other. Rows and reconciliations were inevitable. Perhaps in the hope of getting me to declare myself, Euterpe persuaded her stepmother to ask me to accompany them on a trip to the island of Paros. I was entitled to another week of local leave, and we went. The purpose was to visit a piece of family property on the island; Paros had been without normal communication with the mainland during the four years of the occupation. Even now there were no steamer services. The voyage was to be made by sailing caique, specially chartered by a group of people either having affairs to attend to on Paros, or wanting to attend the well known *paniyiri* of Saint John the Forerunner, which is held at the village of Lefkes on his feast day, 29 August. We were to sail from the Piraeus a few days before that, at nine in the morning. I arranged for a jeep to collect us and by eight o'clock we were all three on the quay of the *kaiki* port. The *Ayios Nikolaos* lay rocking below us in a many-coloured jostle of craft. She was a big, sturdy caique, of traditional lines, with no superstructure above the curving deck except the housing for a small auxiliary engine and a shed-like contraption overhanging the starboard gunwale, which provided communal toilet facilities for all on board. I found her name encouraging, for Saint Nicholas is the patron of sailors, as well as of small boys, pawnbrokers and parish clerks. The *capetanios* was a wiry middle-aged man, with grizzled hair and deeply tanned face. He wore an old jersey and trousers, but no shoes, and resembled the ageing Charlie Chaplin, without the moustache but with four days' growth of beard. A younger man and a boy made up the crew, not counting a stout lady well wrapped in brown, presumed to be the captain's wife.

We bought *koulouria* – quoit-shaped rolls topped with sesame seeds – and ate them in the morning sunshine, while the other passengers arrived in ones and twos. At nine there was still no sign of movement. One traveller was missing and he an important person – an *episimos* – without whom it would have been impolitic to leave. (His name was Crispi, suggesting that he was a descendant of the Crispi family from Verona, who were Dukes of Naxos and Paros five hundred years earlier.) At about ten Mr Crispi condescended to appear, but still nobody embarked. A dispute arose between the *capetanios* and the assistant harbour-master on the matter of life-saving equipment. The total ship's complement was twenty-four; the caique carried three lifebelts and fifteen pairs of primitive water-wings, each consisting of two gourds tied together with string; therefore, the assistant harbour-master argued, even if he stretched a point and conceded that the water-wings might keep one afloat for half an hour, six passengers would still be without any form of lifebelt, and it was against regulations for us to put to sea. There was really no valid counter to this, and it appeared impracticable to acquire extra equipment. The argument dragged on. The day grew steadily hotter. The assistant harbour-master was undermined with cups of coffee and glasses of ouzo, but he was adamant until two o'clock, when he suddenly departed, we all went aboard and the captain cast off. Perhaps a bribe did the trick; perhaps he reckoned that if we perished he could say that he had been threatened by an English officer; perhaps he just wanted his siesta.

The *Saint Nicholas* edged out from its companion caiques, the boy started the engine, which was capable of driving us at about one knot, and we moved at a swan's pace from the inner to the outer harbour and so to the port entrance, where, passing the tiny shrine to the All-Holy Virgin, we earnestly made our intercessions with many signs of the Cross. Once out in the Saronic Gulf we immediately caught a fair breeze. The *meltemia*, those Etesian winds which gave Saint Paul so much trouble on his journey to Rome, were in full blast, and it was this wind, tempered by the shelter of the Attic mainland, which provided our driving force. When the big sail was set, the caique leapt forward like a horse at the starting gate. We sailed steadily south-eastwards down the gulf towards Cape Sounion.

We reached the cape as the sun was setting. The captain announced that he did not intend to venture into the open Aegean in the dark with a high sea running. He put in close to the shore, under the pillars of Poseidon poised far above us, and dropped anchor. Several of us went ashore in the dinghy, reckoning that the ground, however hard, could not be more uncomfortable than the deck and that natural were preferable to nautical sanitary arrangements. So we passed an uneasy night, under the aegis of the sea-god, and at first light were rowed back to the *Saint Nicholas*.

The wind had fallen light during the hours of dark, but as soon as we cleared the cape we met a relentless sea, hunting down from the Hellespont. In the strait between Kea and Kythnos a shoal of flying fish streamed shimmering across the bows. After that the sea was empty except for the occasional lone shearwater, planing along the slopes of the waves on wooden wings. The captain, with one brown foot on the tiller, eased and humoured his craft aslant their untiring advance, while his wife beside him stolidly knitted on two prodigious needles. The movement of the caique was too much for most of the passengers, including Euterpe, who lay in heaps of misery on the deck, holding lemons to their noses and moaning. I wedged myself upright in the stern and held nausea at bay with dry biscuits and small sweet yellow grapes.

All day long we were driven forward by the dynamic interaction of the wind, the sea and the boat. The *meltemi* blew steadily from the same quarter, rising almost to a gale by the afternoon. The sun travelled across the burning, cloudless sky. The waters were ink-dark, with lacework patterns of foam shifting on the surface sheen. The islands of the Cyclades, Syra on the left hand, Seriphos and Siphnos on the right, rose from the haze, passed and slid behind us, tawny as lions. As evening fell, Paros loomed ahead, and we rounded a point to see a line of windmills on the slant of a hill and below them the little white town of Paroikià, in whose harbour we came to rest.

We put up in the town's best hotel. This offered, for one-and-sixpence (7½p) a night, a decent-sized whitewashed room with an iron bedstead, a wooden chair, clean linen and for ablutions an enamelled basin on a table and hanging on the wall above it a copper *niptir* – a water container fitted with a small tap. There were two primitive lavatories. It was all spotless, in this respect matching the whole town. The flagstones of the narrow streets, each picked out with whitewash, looked clean enough to eat off. We ate simply but well in one or other of two tavernas. The town was innocent of tourists or holidaymakers, or of any form of provision for them. There was no sign of mechanically driven vehicles, mules and donkeys being the only means of transport.

The *meltemi* continued to blow all day and every day, swirling round street corners and banging any unfastened door and shutter. We made one or two attempts at swimming, but shelter was hard to find and in the end we gave it up as too disagreeable. We visited the famous Church of a Hundred Doors – the Ekatondopyliani – and made an expedition to the island's miniature version of the Valley of the Butterflies on Rhodes. The trees of the glade are covered by what appear to be grey leaves until alarm makes them fill the air with a whirl of red underwings. The main event of our stay was the *panayiri* at Lefkes. The village is three or four miles from the port, and it was necessary to hire a mule, with its owner, to carry Euterpe's stepmother. We started off after breakfast, accompanied as it seemed by half the population of Paroikia, and climbed past the ancient marble quarries up the winding road to the centre of the island, in a long, scattered procession of men, women, children and animals.

An hour and a half's walk through the burnt browns, yellows and greys of the summer landscape brought us to Lefkes, a large village of crooked lanes and close-packed white houses, huddled against the winter storms on a valley side. Like the town, it gave an impression of exceptional cleanliness. All sharp lines and corners were blurred by innumerable coats of whitewash, which had been recently renewed, as had the edging of the flagstones. The church was crammed with worshippers and we joined the overflow which crowded the little square. It was very hot in the August sunshine. At last, to a jangle of bells, the priest emerged, carrying the icon of the Baptist (as always, portrayed as shaggy in camel skin, equipped with wings, and unkempt of hair and beard) and led off the procession of choir and people. On its devious way it traversed the whole of the village. Saucers of burning incense on many of the window ledges sent a drift of sharply fragrant smoke down the narrow streets. At open doorways kerchiefed old ladies in black gave friends and relatives in the procession the greeting – '*Chronia polla*', 'Many years'.

When the bells announced that the saint was safely home

again, we dispersed and the three of us went to eat our lunch under the trees of an apricot grove outside the village. We had brought with us bread, olives, spicy meat balls, tomatoes, feta cheese and peaches, together with a bottle of red wine, after which not even the hardness of the ground could keep us from sleep. We awoke to the sound of fiddle music. At a small circular dancing place beside the road, a violinist and clarinettist were accompanying a traditional island dance. A single, strong, solid girl in white turned impassively on one spot, her feet moving in a simple basic step. A succession of young men danced with her, each coming forward to hold the corner of the handkerchief in her hand and to vie with the boy before him in the agility of his footwork, the height of his leaps and the springing grace of his body. It was clearly the beginning of a long evening, but the sun was getting low and we had a long way to go, so we had to leave and retrace our steps to town.

At the end of a week the *meltemi* showed no sign of abating. The *capetanios* sent word that the return voyage was, for the time being, impossible, the wind this time not being in our favour. There was no other way of getting off the island, so I sought out the telegraph office and by courtesy of a helpful and efficient operator, was able to let the adjutant know that I was stormbound on Paros. In the event we had to spend a second week there before the wind changed and allowed us to make a comfortable return, with a stop at Syra on the way.

Summer slipped into autumn, the tenderest season of the Greek year. October rain spread a green enamelling of new grass over the parched earth, picked out with pink and white cyclamens and purple, cream and yellow crocuses. Kifissia smelt of pine and our horses came into their own.

The saddle school had come to nothing, but the horses needed exercise and some of us could ride, after a fashion. There was a wide extent of scrub land, intersected by tracks, above Kifissia, and we often rode there on warm golden evenings. My other memories of that autumn are less happy. I was unsettled and saw no clear and painless resolution of the tension between Euterpe and myself. At the beginning of November, my home leave came up. We parted rather miserably, and I asked a friend who knew her to keep in touch with her and with me.

The journey back from the Mediterranean was as different as it could be from that which had taken me there, almost three years earlier. Then I had travelled with the support and comradeship of a fighting unit. We had sailed from the Clyde, as part of a convoy, in the SS *Banfora*, a West Indian banana boat, converted into a troopship of inconceivable awfulness. The convoy made a long detour into the North Atlantic, in very bad weather, before passing through the Straits of Gibraltar and heading for Algeria. We were keyed up by expectation of active service, as well as by apprehension of attack by enemy submarines or aircraft. (One ship of the convoy was in fact sunk, with some loss of life, not far from Algiers.) Now I was alone, feeling like a number among other nameless numbers, herded from a transit camp in Athens on to a ship for Bari and another transit camp, thence by train to a third camp at Milan and finally by train again to a French Channel port. My memory, which, like a sundial, records best the sunlit hours, has rejected all details of that dreary journey, except that we passed through the Alps by night, in a carriage without light or heat, and that at the Swiss frontier the train was boarded by two immaculate officers armed with revolvers. We presumed that they had orders to shoot any fighter for freedom and democracy who might be tempted to set foot on hallowed neutral soil. A rumour was put about – but this may only have been another of those Swiss-Aberdonian jokes – that the Swiss charged the British government one golden sovereign for every man transported across their country.

I had been at home in Edinburgh for little more than a

week when everything changed. Word came that I had been granted an early release from the Forces to return to university. I reported to a demobilisation centre, was issued with an ill-fitting three-piece suit and – 'O tempora, o mores' – a trilby hat, and became a civilian in time for Christmas. At the same time I heard from my friend in Athens that Euterpe had had a letter from her Hans, that he wanted to come back to Greece to marry her, and that she had quite recovered her spirits at the prospect. And so it turned out and the whole matter had a satisfactory ending. It was something that I had stood in for a decent young man.

For the next three years learning the law occupied much of my time and energy, but Greece having engaged my heart, I could not let her slip from my life. I read to fill the gaps in my knowledge of the Greek people and their history, and tried to improve my grasp of the modern language. Half-a-dozen of us, returned warriors who had served in Greece, used to meet once a week in John Mavrogordato's room, to read aloud and translate works in the demotic, such as Venezis's *Aioliki Yi*. But the chance of revisiting the country seemed increasingly remote as the civil war flared up again and created a state of emergency.

Fortune kept intact for me one slender thread of communication. Marily had confided to me a wild fancy that she might one day be able to study at Oxford and I had, equally wildly, said that, if I went back there, I would see what I could do about it. In the event, this amounted to nothing at all, but the least I could do was to keep in touch with her and we carried on an irregular and frivolous correspondence. In the summer of 1947 she wrote to tell me that she was about to come to London with her mother and would spend a few weeks there on holiday before going to study in Switzerland. The first Edinburgh Festival was about to begin. What more natural than to invite her to stay for a few days with my parents and me? She came, and on the station platform, No.

21, I saw that the girl with the comical smile had become Nausicaa's loveliest daughter.

The sun shone. Edinburgh was full of conductors, singers, musicians, writers, painters, dancers, critics and artistic hangers-on. Glyndebourne put on *The Marriage of Figaro*, the Vienna Philharmonic, under Bruno Walter, played Beethoven, and all the world adored Kathleen Ferrier. It was all too much for us. We stood poised to plunge fathoms deep in love. On the next All Fools' Day she agreed to marry me, and not even being taken back by her family to Greece for eight months changed her mind.

So it came about that after nearly four years I was on my way back to Greece, heading for Corfu and destiny at the Saint.

Five

In the year A.D. 325 the Roman emperor Constantine the
Great, having planned a new imperial capital at the old Greek
city of Byzantium, and having proclaimed Christianity as the
state religion of the Empire, decided that the tenets of that
religion ought to be clearly and officially defined. He summoned an ecumenical council, to take place at Nicaea in Asia
Minor and thither, from all parts of the emperor's domin-
ions, from Britain and from Africa, from Spain and Syria and
the heartlands of Greece and Italy, by sailing ship and travelling carriage, by horse or mule or humbly on foot, con-
verged the bishops of the Church Universal.

Among these was the Father-in-God of the obscure diocese
of Trimuthion in Cyprus, by name Spyridion. The story
goes that at a critical point in the Council's pursuit of that
elusive butterfly, the nature of the Godhead, Spyridion produced from beneath his vestments a brick and threw it to the
floor of the church, where it broke. Fire and water sprang
from the fragments of its clay, demonstrating that a trinity of
substances co-existed in the unity of the brick. This miracu-
lous contribution to the making of the Nicene Creed is
Bishop Spyridion's only recorded excursion into theology.
He was, however, known for qualities more important in a
bishop, a saintly simplicity of soul and natural sweetness of
disposition.

Spyridion was the son of a poor shepherd and as a young
man made his living by keeping sheep. After his wife's death
he heard the call to a religious life, became a monk and was
finally consecrated bishop of the very village and district of
his birth and upbringing. He seems to have been endowed
with healing hands and was credited with many cures,

among them that of Constans, Constantine's son, who succeeded his father as emperor. He died in 350, full of years and much loved by his people.

For long after the old bishop's death, men noticed a sweet scent in the neighbourhood of his tomb, and the Church authorities, detecting the odour of sanctity, exhumed his body and found that it had not decomposed. Suitably enshrined, the relic soon became an object of veneration. Prayers for recovery from illness, offered at the shrine, were often effectual. Canonisation inevitably followed and as a saint Spyridion became widely renowned as a worker of healing miracles. (In Orthodox iconography he is represented in episcopal vestments, with a distinctive conical mitre. Visitors to the ancient Agora at Athens can find him depicted in the little church, dedicated to the Holy Apostles, near the south end of the Stoa of Attalus. He appears in fresco on the left-hand pillar of the entrance from the narthex.)

In 632 the Prophet Mohammed died. The armies of Islam at once erupted from Arabia and engulfed the south-eastern provinces of the Byzantine Empire. Cyprus, though an island, did not escape. The Arabs invaded and occupied it in 644. Rather than see the holy body of their saint fall into Saracen hands, the Cypriots allowed him to be transported to Constantinople. Eventually he was installed in the great Church of the Holy Apostles, which once stood at a main road junction in the centre of the city. There, for eight hundred years, Saint Spyridion was a goal of pilgrimage and won an increasing reputation as a thaumaturge.

In 1204 the soldiers of the Fourth Crusade, which had been diverted to Constantinople through the machinations of the Venetians and their blind octogenarian doge, Enrico Dandolo, stormed the walls along the Golden Horn – the first taking of the city in its nine-hundred-year history as capital of the Empire. In one of the most discreditable episodes of European Christendom the soldiers of the Cross looted and raped, and desecrated the churches of their fellow Christians.

Meanwhile, in a shabby deal with the Venetians, their leaders parcelled out the Greek lands of the Byzantine state among themselves. A Flemish emperor was enthroned in the city, while lesser potentates included a northern Italian king of Salonica, a French prince of Achaea and a Burgundian duke of Athens. The Greeks, however, regained Constantinople within sixty years, and Saint Spyridion's body was unscathed by the period of Latin dominance. (The English seem to have sent few knights to the Fourth Crusade. Perhaps the incessant adventuring of the late Richard Lionheart had jaded his barons' appetite for crusading. Perhaps they felt that they had enough on their hands in dealing with his deplorable brother John.)

The main beneficiaries of the Fourth Crusade's diversion were, as they had intended, the Venetians. Their grand aim was to secure a trade route to Egypt, which would enable them to monopolise Europe's commerce with the Far East. For this they needed a string of harbours and naval bases between Venice and Alexandria and their deal with the Crusaders included the right to acquire Corfu, the ports of Modon and Coron in the Peloponnese and the island of Cerigo (as the Franks called Kythera, where Aphrodite first rose from the foam), between the Greek mainland and Crete. To these the Venetians very quickly added their greatest prize, the island of Crete itself. It was intended to form part of Boniface of Montferrat's kingdom of Salonica, but the marquis was so short of cash that he was happy to sell it to the doge and relieve himself of the expense of governing such remote territory.

Venice took over Corfu, but found that she lacked the resources to hold the island and was forced to cede possession (without renouncing her claim) to Michael Angelos, the Greek Despot of Epirus. It enjoyed a period of considerable prosperity for sixty years under the despotat, and then passed to the Angevin dynasty of Naples. The Angevins, who harboured Greek imperial ambitions, introduced a feudal sys-

66

tem, on Western lines, dividing the island into baronies which were allotted to Italian or Provençal barons and reducing the peasant population virtually to the status of serfs. Even the gypsies of Corfu became vassals of a particular lord, their service being the obligation to gather and sing to him once a year. The Angevin administration was tolerant of the Jewish religion and a sizeable Jewish community established itself on the island.

This regime lasted for a hundred and twenty years. It was, on the whole, beneficent, but became unstable because of civil wars in the Neapolitan state. During the fourteenth century the Venetians twice tried to regain Corfu and finally, in 1386, their chance came. The islanders, weary of misgovernment and the depredations of pirates, sent a six-man deputation, part Italian, part Greek and part Jewish, to Venice, to request the Most Serene Republic to take over the island. So began four centuries of Venetian rule, with its powerful influence on the economy, architecture and social structure of Corfu.

Controlling as it does the mouth of the Adriatic, which is also the shortest sea crossing between Italy and Greece, Corfu was of prime strategic importance to the Venetians. It became in time their principal naval base and the headquarters of the *Proveditore generale del Levante,* always a Venetian, who held office for three years and whose arrival was an occasion of immense pomp. The little harbour, below the northern walls of the Old Fortress, known as the Mandrakion and now used by small craft, once sheltered the war galleys of the republic. The government found useful the aristocratic society which they inherited from the Angevins. The noble Neapolitan and Greek families were allowed to keep their estates and were encouraged to be loyal to Venice by having minor official posts allotted to them. The 'Golden Book' – the Libro d'Oro – was instituted, in whose pages no one's name could be entered who was engaged in trade. Thus was perpetuated a privileged class, enjoying an illusion of importance, sending their sons to be awarded degrees at the University of Padua, speaking Venetian as fluently as Greek and with little in common, except the Orthodox religion, with the peasantry who worked on their land.

On 29 May 1453, after a long and bruising siege, the soldiers of the Ottoman sultan, Mehmet II, breached the land walls of Constantinople. The emperor, the eleventh and last of the Constantines, died fighting in a vain attempt to save the city. Byzantium, the second Rome, preserver of classical learning and Christian doctrine for over a thousand years, was usurped by the Moslem descendants of nomads from Central Asia.

Little enough was saved from the debacle – so little that Spyridion's rescue looks like the result of a decision by the saint to justify his reputation as a worker of miracles. One George Kalochairetis, a citizen of substance who was himself a priest, removed from the church the bodies both of Spyridion and of a less renowned saint, Theodora Augusta, hid them in bales of hay, loaded them on mules and in merchant's disguise drove his sacred freight out of the city. Their journey took them westwards through Thrace and Macedonia and over the Pindus range into the steep land of Epirus. From there he succeeded in shipping his strange cargo to Christian territory in Corfu, where the two saints were given a resting place in one of the town's churches. The year was now 1456.

George Kalochairetis deserves, and got, high credit for his devotion and enterprise. His name is commemorated in the little street, parallel to that of the saint on the other side of his church. He clearly believed that he was further entitled to some sort of proprietorial right over the two saintly bodies, for on his death he bequeathed Spyridion to his two elder sons, Philip and Luke, and Theodora to Mark the youngest. In 1483, either out of public spirit or because the maintenance of Saint Theodora was more trouble and expense than she was worth, Mark made her over to the community. Her

68

remains were eventually laid in the cathedral of Corfu and are there to this day.*

Luke Kalochairetis returned to Epirus, where he became a priest at the town of Arta, and the effective control of Saint Spyridion remained with the eldest brother, Philip. In 1489 he went to Venice, represented to the doge that a saint of such standing should be housed in the capital and was granted letters authorising him to arrange for his transfer from Corfu. By this time, however, Spyridion was so much revered by the Corfiots for his miracles of healing and other benefits that there was a public outcry and lamentation, which persuaded Philip not to carry out his plan. The saint was transferred to the church of Saint Michael the Archangel, in the district known as Vriovouni – the Hill of the Hebrews – which was the old Jewish quarter of Corfu town.

Twenty or so years later, Philip Kalochairetis died, survived by his widow Maria and one daughter, Asimina, who fell heir to her father's share of the saint. Luke, who was childless, in 1512 made over his share to his niece. Asimina had become a considerable matrimonial catch. The husband found for her was a Corfiot named Stamatis (more commonly known, Venetian-wise, as Stamatello) Bulgari. They were married in 1521 and by deed of dowry Maria made over to her son-in-law, along with the ordinary items of furniture, linen and silver, a piece of land and the relics of the blessed miracle-worker Spyridion.

It cannot have been other than an arranged match and Asimina's mother would only have been satisfied with a man of social standing who was able to provide for her. Contemporary documents are lost, but family tradition is clear that Stamatello was the great-grandson of one Stefano de' Bulgari, who had settled in Corfu about sixty years earlier. He is said to have been a descendant of a powerful Bulgarian noble

* Theodora was the wife of the iconoclast emperor Theophilus. She was canonised for her part in the restoration of the icons after her husband's death. She does not inspire much enthusiasm.

named Eleazar, and to have left Bulgaria, after that country was conquered by the Turks in 1393, to have been accepted at the court of the Greek despots of Mistra, to have married a Greek wife and to have escaped to Corfu in the wake of the Despot Thomas Paleologos (brother of the Emperor Constantine XI) when the Ottomans overran the Peloponnese in 1460. He got permission from the authorities to make his home in Corfu and established a successful business.

Stamatello lost little time in taking advantage of his marriage. In 1527 he obtained official permission to build a new church, to be dedicated to St Spyridion, and six years later sought authority to transfer the saint's remains from the church of St Michael to his own church. This was, not unnaturally, strongly opposed by the community, who were against the idea that a saint of the Church Universal – especially one whom they had taken to their hearts – should be in the custody of a private citizen in his private chapel. Argument on behalf of Maria Kalochairetis and the syndics of the community was heard by the governor, sitting as a court, and on 22 November 1531 judgment was given in Maria's favour. Thereafter the body of the saint was carried with due ceremony to the new Bulgari church (not the present–day church of the Saint.)

In 1537 the Turkish forces under the famous admiral Khaireddin Barbarossa launched a full-scale invasion of Corfu, making their landing at Gouvia Bay. They occupied and ravaged the whole island, devastating its agriculture and killing or capturing nine-tenths of the population. The only part of the capital which held out was the Old Fortress, which was the military headquarters and principal stronghold, and the saint was taken there for safety. The siege lasted for many weeks, with terrible hardship. At last, Barbarossa, realising that without the fortress he could not hold the island and seeing that his troops were suffering from hunger and disease, withdrew his forces and a major threat to Western Christendom was averted.

Stamatello Bulgari died in 1566, survived by Asimina and by four sons, two of whom were priests. In 1571 Asimina made a will, bequeathing the saint to her sons and their descendants in perpetuity, but only upon the strict condition that they maintain the church and conduct all its services, on pain of incurring a mother's curse and being totally disinherited if they should fail to do so.

The fear of a repetition of the invasion of 1537 persuaded the Venetians that the town must be adequately fortified. Work on this was begun in the 1580s and involved the demolition of many buildings, including Stamatello Bulgari's church. Accordingly a new church, of rich splendour, was erected on the site where it stands to the present day. A family house was also built, adjoining the west end of the church. From then on the Bulgari family faithfully carried out the terms of Asimina's will and managed, for more than three centuries, to uphold their monopoly of the saint, in the face of various attempts by the community to displace them. The monopoly was both honorific and valuable. By the end of the sixteenth century, Spyridion had come to be regarded as more than a revered benefactor and intercessor on behalf of individuals. He was unquestionably the patron of the whole island. He was credited with having saved its people from starvation in a season of dearth, by appearing in a vision to the captain of a grain ship and directing him to divert his cargo to Corfu. In celebration of this miracle the saintly body was, and still is, carried in procession through the town on the Great Saturday before Easter of every year. (Similar processions were instituted on Palm Sunday and the first Sunday in November, to commemorate two occasions in the seventeenth century when the saint was believed to have halted outbreaks of plague. The procession of 11 August honours the assistance given by him to Count Schulemburg's troops in defeating the Turkish attempt on the island in 1716.)

These litanies and other feasts of the saint were attended by

71

dignitaries of the Orthodox and Roman Catholic Churches and from all branches of the administration and armed forces. The Bulgaris were at the heart of it all. For reasons of self-preservation they cultivated good relations with the Venetian rulers. They were listed in the Libro d'Oro, acquired landed property and, over and above, enjoyed a comfortable surplus from the revenue of their church. The constant, generous offerings of the faithful were more than sufficient for its maintenance. Finally, after the Turkish attack of 1716, the Venetian state conferred on the family – along with others – the title of count, usable by all its male members, in recognition of their services in the defence of the town.

By this time Venice was sinking into frivolous decline. In 1797 the Serenissima surrendered without a struggle to Napoleon Bonaparte. The *Enetokratia* of Corfu was over. Soldiers of the French Revolution arrived and burnt the Golden Book, to the applause of the common people. They also abolished Sundays and feast days and insulted the saint. Their early popularity quickly evaporated and even the peasants were glad to see them go, to be replaced by the chimera of a Russo-Turkish condominium. The Russians, being Orthodox in religion, venerated Saint Spyridion, and the fortunes of the Bulgaris revived. When the French returned a few years later it was in Imperial guise. They administered well, built the Liston arcade on the Plateia in the style of the Rue de Rivoli and left the aristocracy unmolested. For fifty years from 1814, Corfu and the other Ionian islands were administered by the British, technically as a protectorate, in practice as a colony. They treated the islanders with their usual patronising disdain of foreigners, but the aristocratic principle was upheld. Things went on as before.

In 1864 the British government ceded the Ionian islands to the young kingdom of the Hellenes. After an interval of six hundred years Corfu was again part of a Greek state. The rest of the Greeks had mixed feelings towards these Italianised compatriots, whose foreign domination, however tiresome, had spared them the tempering fire of the Turkish occupation and denied them the glories of revolution and liberation. Venetian titles did not impress and were not officially recognised. The Bulgaris had, in effect, lost their power base. It could only be a matter of time before they lost their privileged possession of the saint. Not without a stubborn litigation, he passed into public ecclesiastical custody in 1925.

The last of the line of family priests instituted by Asimina, Stephanos Bulgari, was born in 1881. A boy of artistic talent, he was studying in Rome to be a painter when his father decided to give up the priesthood and go to live in Nice with an American inamorata. He sent for Stephanos, who obediently returned to Corfu, was ordained, and took up his family duty. Although he lost the saint, he remained as his priest until his death in 1950. His son, Spiro, as a nineteen-year-old law student, married in 1925 the even younger Catherine Pappou, member of an Athenian family with strong political connections, and granddaughter of Dimitrios Rallis, a vehement Royalist and anti-Veneizelist, who was several times Prime Minister of Greece. He was descended from the old Constantinopolitan family, probably of Norman origin, whose name was a corruption of Raoul. They had close connections with the Imperial court of Byzantium, and some held high office under the Ottoman sultans. Dimitrios's father had escaped from Constantinople as a child, after his father had been decapitated by the sultan on suspicion of being involved in the Greek revolution of 1821.

This premature alliance of disparate cultures broke up only too quickly, but not before it had produced the acute, humorous, gentle, warm-hearted girl who, unaccountably, was prepared to come to live with me at the far end of Europe.

73

Six

Ian, my best man, came with me to collect her. Both travel and accommodation were beset with problems in 1949, and bedevilled by British currency restrictions and Greek governmental controls. Invitations to the wedding would have looked like a cry for presents rather than personal attendance, and my father's health made the journey impossible for my parents. So Ian was my only supporter.

The flight to Athens lasted almost twelve hours. The twin screws drove us at the, then, dashing air-speed of 180 mph, and at a height which enabled one to distinguish homely details of the landscape such as roads and houses. There were two stops for refuelling. The first of these was at Nice airport, which then sported a bijou landing strip practically on the Mediterranean beach. We were all escorted to a garden of palm trees and scarlet hibiscus, in which coffee was served at small tables round an oval goldfish pool. (It is nearly impossible now, in the impersonal, commercial purgatory of Heathrow or Gatwick, to credit the solicitude with which passengers used to be treated. Air travel was still exceptional for unimportant people – we were, in time, just half-way between Amy Johnson and Concorde – and we were shepherded and cosseted on the assumption, more often than not correct, that most of us had never flown before, and were scared out of our wits.) The second stop was at Rome's Ciampino aerodrome, which looked and sounded like a building site directed by the Marx Brothers with a cast of thousands.

We pottered down the west coast of Italy, across the instep of its boot, and out over the Ionian, where, as Lawrence Durrell remarked, 'the blue begins', signalling the subtle change of light between the western and eastern Mediterranean. We flew on, weary now, into the onrush of the twilight. Then it was dark and I felt a tightening of excitement as the lights of Athens swung up to receive me back. The remembered hot breath of a July evening struck my face at the aircraft door. I had the feeling that Greece and I had never been meant to be separated.

We spent two nights with Marily's Athenian grandmother before setting off for Corfu. We went by boat. There was not, so far as I can remember, any question of taking a plane for this part of the journey, though it would have been possible to do so, travelling in an honourably retired and roughly converted military Dakota. These sturdy vehicles used to skim close to the Greek mountaintops and bucket in the summer up-currents of hot air, giving the sensation of a bus-ride over rough country. As seasoned voyagers may remember, Corfu aerodrome was much smaller then, and the cosy terminal building lay on the opposite side of the runway from the present one, in which thousands of British holidaymakers have happy memories of queuing through the night. The only plane was that from Athens, and the passengers were cared for by a nice girl called Mary, who soothed and reassured the elderly village couples – he in heavy dark suit, she in wide peasant skirt and white head kerchief – setting off in the new flying machine, laden with baskets of cheese, figs and nuts and cardboard boxes tied with string, to visit the grandchildren in Athens.

The other mainstay of the establishment was a stout elderly lady in a white overall coat, who stumped out across the tarmac with pail and broom to make the aircraft presentable for passengers. They meanwhile sat on the open verandah, till the door of the crew's quarters opened, the pilot emerged, wiping froth from his moustaches, and called 'Let's go', and led the procession to the foot of the ladder. But all this ended long ago, when they lengthened the runway almost as far as Mouse Island, and then built hotels and apartments alongside

75

it on the Canoni peninsula, so that the rich and famous could have Boeings on their balconies with their breakfast.

I was not to sample these pleasures for some years yet. In 1949 it was widely held in Greece that if God had intended men to fly he would have constructed them with wings. The proper way to go to Corfu was by one of the regular services of ships which plied from the Piraeus on most days of the week – *Angelica, Mykali, Frinton,* and others – providing the ports of the Ionian and its islands with their principal communication. Besides, it is not only more exciting to approach an island for the first time by sea; it is also more respectful, for it is the sea which gives each island its individual quality and its superiority over dull and vulgar mainlanders.

The name of our steamer has gone from me, but she had, I remember, a fine brass bell and a plate inscribed with the information that she had been built on the Clyde as a ferryboat between Vancouver and Victoria. We sailed late in the evening and I must have slept soundly through the canal and gulf of Corinth, for my first memory is of being awakened in the dawn by the rush of the anchor chain, and seeing a range of golden hills slide across the cabin porthole. It was the bay of Sami in Cephallonia, our first port of call. We were at anchor some little way off from the small harbour, and passengers and their luggage were embarked and disembarked by lighter. This used to be common all over the Ionian and Aegean. The operation was always frenetic, in the case of large, hysterical female travellers theatrical, and in rough weather perilous, but seldom fatal.

The decks were crowded with soldiers of the Greek Army, still equipped with British-style uniforms. I took them to be returning from leave in Athens to the war front in the northwest of the country. The sight of them gave reality to the knowledge that the civil war, of whose bloody beginning I had been a witness, was still in progress five years later. After the thwarting of their coup in Athens, ELAS regrouped in the mountainous north. They were able to obtain supplies

76

there from the Communist states across the frontiers and they also took many children from Greek villages and sent them out to be suitably indoctrinated. Eventually the government, still with British (and later American) support, was obliged to launch a full military campaign to dislodge what was no less than a hostile army on its territory. Hard fighting continued during 1947 and 1948 and it was not until the summer of 1949 that the intractable remnant of ELAS was pinned down on the harsh heights of the Grammos mountains on the Albanian frontier. The soldiers on our ship looked fit and confident, as if knowing that final victory was near – if there can ever be said to be a victory in civil war. The bitterness and the reprisals, by both sides, of that unhappy time left scars which are still not wholly healed.

From Sami we passed up the channel between Cephallonia and Ithaca towards the almost-island of Lefkada. The morning was completely still and soon became very hot and hazy. The ship moved as if enclosed within a huge pearl. From the narrow waterway which cuts the isthmus, trees and houses appeared to dance and shimmer like a mirage. This Ionian world was a Greece that I had not experienced on the Aegean side. We stopped at the port of Lefkada, still being restored from the severe damage of the previous year's earthquake, and headed north to the uninviting town of Preveza. Most of the soldiery disembarked, leaving the boat quiet and half empty.

There followed a leg of about thirty miles to Parga, the next town on the mainland. Midday approached. It grew steadily hotter and hazier and there was a feel of thunder in the air. Somewhere to the right ran the coast of Epirus, invisible in the luminous obscurity. Floating in an opalescent limbo, with only the unruffled flatness of the sea to contemplate, I began to doubt the sanity, if not the reality, of the whole enterprise. What in the world was I doing, what fearful risks taking, borne inexorably towards an unknown island, with full highland dress in my suitcase, to marry a girl

77

I had not seen, and had scarcely spoken to, for eight months? In the autumn Marily's mother had summoned her back to Athens on pretext of family duties, which we suspected to be the cover for a design to give us time for cool reflection. To make matters worse, the Berlin airlift had just begun and there was much talk of a Third World War, this time with Russia on the other side.

I went ahead on the principle that the worst hardly ever happens. I 'passed advocate' and started to practise at the Bar in Edinburgh. I bought what I trusted was a suitable flat for our first home. I even obtained from my bishop (at the insistence of the Church authorities in Corfu) a certificate of good moral character, impeccable orthodoxy of belief and regular church attendance. This document, which began re-gally 'WE KENNETH', and ended with so many seals and strips of purple ribbon that it resembled an Imperial Rescript ('Continentals always like lots of sealing-wax,' said the bishop), presumably lies yet, with its Greek translation, in the bowels of the Metropolitan Office of the Diocese of Corfu and Paxos. Marily and I also corresponded with pas-sionate regularity, and very occasionally wasted much time in trying, first, to get through to each other and, second, to hear a single word that was said, on the erratic trunk call system between Scotland and Greece. After all that, what if we didn't recognise each other? What if she didn't like me any more? Or I her? I sought out Ian and talked of more mundane things.

Parga was as picturesque as Preveza had not been. Here we were entering historic Corfiot waters, for in the Venetian era Parga was one of two mainland dependencies, not subject to Turkish rule. (The other, further north, was Bouthroton, or Butrinto, valued for its fisheries, which lies in modern Alba-nia.) The Pargites were noted smugglers and gun-runners and probably a great nuisance to the Ottoman authorities, who nevertheless seem to have done little to expel the Vene-to-Corfiot garrison. It was unlucky for them that Corfu became part of the British Protectorate. The first Lord High Commissioner, Sir Thomas ('King Tom') Maitland, adopting a loose interpretation of the word 'protection', agreed to sell Parga to Ali Pasha, the governor of Ioannina. Ali Pasha was nominally subject to the sultan but in practice an autonomous tyrant. His captivating charm of manner was matched by the consistent treachery and cruelty of his deeds, and the people of Parga realised that they were done for once they fell into his power. Losing no time, they evacuated themselves, their hens and their icons to Corfu and other islands. Only many years later, when Epirus at last became part of the Greek kingdom, were their descendants able to return home.

If I had known this at the time, I might have performed some act of penance on the deck. As it was, I admired the jumbled little town on its peninsula from the bay where, as at Sami, our ship lay at anchor and enjoyed the hubbub of passengers and their gear being unloaded and loaded. We then set a straight course up the gulf to Corfu. Soon one could make out the white cliffs at the end of the island's long tail, and then, one by one, the mountains of the east-coast villages – Chlomos, Benitses and Gastouri – all draped, in spite of the heat, with gauzy scarves of cloud, my first sight of the dampness with which Corfu can wrap itself even at the height of summer. Finally, out of the heavy blur of the afternoon, there materialised the two humps of the fortress – the twin peaks, the Korypho, which gave the name of Corfu to the old island of Kerkyra.

Between us and the town lay, like enormous ducks brooding on the glassy deep, a line of grey warships, white ensigns limp at the stern. Marily had told me that the British Mediterranean Fleet, commanded by Lord Louis Mountbatten, was paying a courtesy visit to Corfu, but it had not occurred to me that it might be strung out across the mouth of Garitsa Bay to receive me like a guard of honour. After the initial surprise, the presence of those strong ships with their menacing guns seemed both reassuring and quite natural. It had not yet struck home in Britain that the empire on which the sun never set, and which formed part of our mental furniture, was collapsing around us; that dreamy afternoon's apparition beautifully preserved the illusion that we were still maintaining the Pax Britannica throughout the Seven Seas. If anyone had told me that twenty years later the American Sixth Fleet would be lying off the Piraeus, to give moral support to a junta of Colonels, I would have supposed him mad.

We rounded Capo Sidero, the point at the end of the fort, and anchored in the bay of the old port, used nowadays by the Igoumenitsa car ferries. (The New Port – the Neon Limani – with its customs building, which handles all other shipping, did not then exist.) I do not remember thinking it odd – I now see it as endearingly typical – that Corfu should possess an airport, but no harbour deep enough for island steamers to tie up at the quay. My mind was in too much of a flurry for reflections, as I scanned the flotilla of small boats approaching across the water. In one of them sat a girl with her father, and as soon as I looked down into her face, I reckoned that everything was going to be all right.

Seven

Nine years of war had scarred Corfu and destroyed its way of life. The town was badly damaged by aerial bombing – the only city in Greece, I think, except the Piraeus, to have suffered in this way. The Italians dropped bombs when they finally entered Greece and took over Corfu. After the fall and death of Mussolini and Italy's change of sides, the Germans naturally took steps to extend their occupation to those regions held, till then, by their former allies. Italy, which harboured a persistent fantasy that Corfu belonged to it by right, refused to withdraw her troops. The Germans were obliged to mount an armed attack on the island, which included a heavy bombardment of the capital. (By a stroke of historical irony, they also destroyed the Kaiserbrucke – the elegant stone bridge over the coastal road at Perama, built by the emperor Wilhelm II as an access to the Imperial landing-stage. Hitler's tanks advancing along the road found the bridge too narrow to pass through and blasted it with their guns.) The RAF also dropped a few bombs to hurry the German Army on its way in 1944.

Many houses were destroyed. The old Campiello district, above the sea walls of the Mourayia, was a scene of devastation, and nearly every street showed gaps in its buildings, a few of which remain to this day. The opera house was ruined, and fire gutted the principal hotel, the Bella Venezia. The fine library bequeathed to Corfu by Lord Guilford (the eccentric peer who became Greek Orthodox, and founded the Ionian Academy where the students were required to wear classical chitons) was also burned out. All these had to be demolished.

Even after 1944 a state of war continued between Greece

and Albania (not officially ended until 1987). The Albanians were regarded as an active threat because of the aid which they gave to ELAS during the civil war. They also celebrated their independence from occupation, and demonstrated their level of civilisation, by laying mines in the narrows between their coast and Corfu. As a result two Royal Navy destroyers using the channel were damaged, with the loss of forty lives. The channel was closed to civilian shipping until well into the 1950s and ships coming from Italy had to make the detour round the south end of the island. More inconveniently for the inhabitants, the whole of the north of the island was declared a prohibited frontier area. Military checkpoints were set up on the main roads to the north, at Pyryi and the Trompeta pass, making it impossible, without special permission, to visit the villages of Mount Pantocrator, or the northern coasts. Gone, perhaps for ever, were the boar-hunts and duck-shoots on the shores of Albania, enjoyed by Corfiot sportsmen in the days of the Turks and of good King Zog.

There was a positive military presence in the town. The Old Fortress, little used since the departure of the British Army in 1864, became the headquarters and barracks of a Greek training establishment for army recruits. Each morning the massive gates, and the bridge across the moat of the *contra-fossa*, disgorged squad after squad of young men in full kit, with packs and rifles, who marched out of the town with martial song to the training areas at Potamos, returning at evening after an arduous day in the summer sun. Their instructors were advised by members of a British Military Mission stationed in the town. This, and a Police Mission – gamely struggling to convert the Greek policeman into a replica of the London bobby – were the final relics of an involvement in Greek affairs which had lasted since October 1944.

No sooner had Ian and I disembarked than we were told that we would have to wear our kilts that same evening, for a party at the BMM officers' mess. Marily had been one of the guests, a few evenings earlier, at a cocktail party given by Mountbatten in his flagship. Told that she was expecting her Scottish fiancé, with his best man, both equipped with tartan, he insisted that she bring us to the BMM party given in his honour, and promised to supply a Royal Marine piper to play for us. So it came about. On our first night in Corfu we drank kilted in an Analipsi garden, under the eye of the Admiral of the Fleet, and later steered Corfiot ladies through an eightsome reel to music supplied by a piper in full highland garb.

The German occupation had affected the island's population in one significant respect. The Jewish colony, settled, during the Angevin period, mainly from the Levant, was augmented under the Venetians by an influx of Sephardim from Spain. Their total number grew to about 5,000 – perhaps a fifth of the whole population of the town – with two synagogues, an Eastern and a Western. It was not a particularly prosperous community. Wheeler and others record that they were treated with considerable animosity by the Orthodox Greeks, especially during Holy Week and Easter. However, they survived, mostly as gold- and silversmiths, metal-workers, dealers in all types of materials, cleaners and washerwomen, into the 1930s. Marily remembers their Sabbath outings to Garitsa, where the bay was covered with boatloads of families, the women dressed in very bright colours, all talking at once and calling loudly from boat to boat.

During one year, between 1943 and 1944, the Germans removed every member of this ancient community. Only a handful ever came back, and no more than a couple of Jewish businesses remain in the old Evraiki, the Hebrew quarter.

Readers of Lawrence and Gerald Durrell's books know pre-war Corfu as a gentle, old-fashioned backwater. A decade of shortages and restrictions had only served to set back its progress towards modernity. Electricity had reached very

few of the villages. Private telephones were almost unknown. Because of disuse, lack of replacements and shortage
of petrol, there was scarcely a single private motor-car on the
roads. The road system itself, possibly the British Protectorate's most efficient legacy, was steadily disintegrating from
lack of repair. A fleet of increasingly ancient buses maintained a valiant, but slow and uncomfortable, service between town and country. Failing the bus, the only means of
mechanical transport lay in the corps of veteran taxis. The
youngest of these dated from 1936. A fair proportion were
long roomy touring cars from the 1920s, with canvas hoods
which could be folded back and horns operated by squeezing
a rubber bulb. The doyen was a Mercedes Benz of enormous
length, one of a number owned by the Kaiser and used for
carrying the royal household and guests from the jetty up to
the Achilleion palace at Gastouri, or on excursions to watch
the sunset at Peleka with oysters and champagne.

To be wafted in one of these equipages, on a narrow road
winding through the unruly trunks and freckled shade of the
olive groves, was an experience different from driving on a
modern motorway not in degree but in quintessence. The
road surfaces seldom permitted a speed greater than twenty
miles per hour. Further, the drivers were in the habit, in
order to save fuel, of turning off the engine on any gradient
in their favour, however slight, and coasting almost to a
standstill before letting the gears kick the motor into life. So
one lurched in majestic silence from pothole to pothole,
announcing one's approach only by the wake of white dust
which floated behind the taxi. At intervals one met small
groups of country women, brown-faced and barefoot, moving to or from their fields, some sitting sideways on donkeys,
some leading mules laden with fodder or firewood, some
walking very erect, with movement only from the hips so as
to keep steady the burdens balanced on their heads. At the
sound of the horn they would draw in to the roadside,
pulling the corner of a kerchief over nose and mouth against

the car's dust. If we returned late, bats swerved and squeaked above our chariot as it rolled down into town in the violet gloaming.

The whole island, both town and country, gave the impression of having altered hardly at all for a hundred years. In Athens, the occupation and civil war had seemed no more than a temporary hitch in the city's growth and business activity. In Corfu there was little or no sign of new houses, or of the repair of old ones. The villages were picturesque, with their jumble of tiled roofs and the faded pink and yellow wash of the walls and arcades and outside stairways, but it was a melancholy, crumbling charm and too often there was a feeling of listlessness, born of a shortage of money and a lack of opportunity for the young men.

The land was given over almost entirely to agriculture of an age-old character – the huge olive estates, harvested by picking the fruit from the ground where it had fallen, and the small fields and gardens of the villagers, usually tilled manually with the mattock. The concept of a Mediterranean island as a holiday resort was still far in the future. Outside the town, there were three hotels – the Tourist Pavilion at Paleocastritsa, the Mega at Ypsos, and the Spinoula family's Avra hotel at Benitses – all small and simple, with elementary plumbing. The only hotel of any size in the town, since the destruction of the Bella Venezia, was the Astir, beside the old port, and there were also two *pensions*, the St Georges and the Pension Suisse, both with an Edwardian flavour. The shops were one-family, and often one-man, businesses dealing in the necessities and minor luxuries of living. The only shops which might be remotely classed as 'touristic' were those near the Saint in which pilgrims could buy candles and religious objects.

The town wore an expression of decent sobriety. The narrow streets – the *kandounia* – especially, in the central shopping area of the Piazza, the cake-shops and the cafés along the Plateia, were full of middle-aged gentlemen in suits and middle-aged ladies in hats. Since everybody knew everybody else, there was much raising of homburgs and shaking of hands and inquiries about each other's, and a great many other people's, affairs. The shopkeepers knew all their customers. This led to lively conversation, both private and general, taking precedence over the speedy transaction of business. (The ease and good humour of communication across the widest divides of class and wealth has always been for me one of the most attractive features of Greek society.) Country folk from the villages, and workpeople generally, tended to have business in the commercial quarter round Sarocco Square, but many did not care to leave town without paying a visit to the saint, and there was a constant devout traffic to and from the church.

The wedding day was not for a couple of weeks after our arrival, so Ian and I had time in which to take in this cosy world of the *chora*. We stayed with Marily's father and stepmother, and their two young sons, in a flat close to the Mourayia. Marily was living with her mother, her twin brothers Nicky and Stevie and her half-sister, in a pleasant old house overlooking the Ano Spianada (upper esplanade). From its terrace there was a direct view of the Old Fortress, the esplanade's flower beds and tree-lined paths, the Victorian bandstand and the elegant rotunda erected, so it read, by the grateful citizens (though in lapidary inscriptions tongue may be kept in cheek) in memory of their old tyrant Tom Maitland. Marily's grandfather, Papa Stephano, and grandmother were in residence in the old house beside the church.

In the mornings we went swimming, usually as a family party. We used to go down to the *contra-fossa* by the steps from the little Mandrakina church (which looks like a dwarfish offspring of the Saint) and there hire a boat, with boatman. Our regular Charon was the burly Napoleon, whose fiery face suggested that the brandy was named after him. He would row us – standing, facing the bow and pushing on the oars, in the Corfiot manner – past the Mandraki harbour and below the massive walls of the fort to the point of Capo Sidero. There we bathed in a small rocky cove, under the regard of a carved Lion of St Mark, whose ferocious features had been reduced by time and the elements to an amiable grin. We had the rocks to ourselves. It seemed to be the traditional family *plage*, for Marily has an early memory of her leg being caught there by an octopus's tentacle when she was very small.

On the voyage back, her brother Stevie, an excellent swimmer, dived for sea-urchins. We came to land with up to a dozen of these balls of purplish-black spines. These accompanied us, together with towels and other swimming gear, across the Plateia cricket ground to one of the cafés, where we ordered ouzo, bread and knives. By scooping out the orange interior of the urchins we created a sea-flavoured *mezè* to accompany our drink. The cafés were apparently accustomed to such eccentricities, for they never objected or tried to charge us corkage.

We never again, after that summer, swam off Capo Sidero. The following year a pretty and popular girl – of good family too – was eaten by a shark before the eyes of her boyfriend, when they were swimming out to sea from the civic *plage* at Mon Repos. The tragedy deeply shocked and alarmed Corfu society. For many years few ventured out far from any beach and there were frequent fancied sightings of sinister fins, and false alarms of '*Karkharias, karkharias!*' (Sharks are not known to breed in the Ionian. The individual fish which appear from time to time are generally held to have entered the Mediterranean by following ships through the Suez Canal. If there have been any sightings in Corfiot waters in recent years, they are not mentioned in the holiday tour operators' brochures.)

Afternoons were very hot and of extraordinary length. The Greek word for afternoon is *apoyevma*, which means afterlunch, and since lunch in Corfu seldom began before two o'clock and demanded a decent siesta, or *bizolo*, for digestion, the afternoon, as a period for activity, did not get under way until about 5.30. As the sun went down, it merged imperceptibly into the *vradhaki,* the 'little evening'.

The afternoon was, and is, the time for the formal social call, the *visita*. It is acceptable for the guests to arrive anything up to an hour and a half after the time at which the visit has been arranged. A small gift of chocolates, or the like, is offered, and received with rapture. Cake, with tea, coffee or lemonade, is served. A cake made by the hostess herself leads to elaborate compliments and an exchange of recipes. The next hour, or hour and a half, is devoted to an exploration of the births, deaths, marriages, divorces and inter-relationships of the company's respective families, friends and acquaintances. Any serious exchange of ideas is not considered in good taste. When all possible topics of common interest have been exhausted, the guests indicate that they will soon have to be leaving, *siga-siga* – 'slowly-slowly'. Such untimely haste is deprecated by the hostess and this ritual exchange is repeated two or three times over the next twenty minutes, at the end of which the visitors usually depart. When guests overstay their welcome, this is called an 'Armenian visit'.

The ladies who visited the house on the esplanade to inspect me were well-intentioned but, as far as I was concerned, Armenian. It takes years of practice for a non-Corfiot to acquire the skill of considering boredom as a fine art. Fortunately, Marily and I had some afternoons to ourselves, which we used in savouring the gentle unhurried pleasures of the town. We needed nothing more than to walk among its restful beauty, or to be in love and drinking ginger beer under the trees of the Plateia, while a thousand swifts, high above us, dashed screaming about the fading sky. Or we might hire a *carotsa* – the *carotses* of those days were sober working cabs, not tourist traps bedecked with pom-poms and funny hats for the horses – and drive, with soft clopping of hooves and tinging of the bell, along the leafy road to

Kanoni. This sported just a *kafeneion* and the single old cannon which gives the place its name ('One Gun Point' on the old nautical charts), and of course the celebrated view of Pondikonisi – Mouse Island – and the Vlachernai nunnery, with its islet and causeway. To make the excursion to Kanoni and to linger over that prospect, sweetening it with a spoonful of vanilla or a cup of coffee, was a traditional Corfiot renewal of the spirit.

One afternoon there was a cricket match on the Plateia ground, between the cafés and the fort. The game at that time was being kept alive with a struggle, because of the state of decay of bats, balls and pads, none of which had been replaced since the war. But the keenness was there. Small boys could often be found playing cricket in the *kandounia*, with a soft ball and improvised bat and a wicket chalked on a wall. One of the town clubs was the 'Byron'. I believe the poet would have appreciated that memorial more than all the busts and inscriptions adorning Greek provincial public places. Sometimes I fancied I saw his shade sneak a limping single from an artful *sottogamba*★ at the palace end.

Cricket, as is fairly well known, was introduced by the English during the Protectorate, was adopted by the local inhabitants and has been played ever since. Ginger beer, prepared from a secret Victorian recipe, is the only other obvious British legacy to the island, unless one counts the two bars at the Old Port – Dirty Dick's and The Spoty Dog (*sic*) which were presumably given their names by roistering Jack Tars. The Palace of St Michael and St George, the statues and monuments, the road system and the urban water supply, have no specifically British stamp. However, tucked away off a side-road to the south of the town is a spot, sought out by only a handful of the thousands of British tourists who crowd Corfu all summer, which evokes that anomalous era more poignantly than palace or togaed effigy. Beneath the tombstones of the British Cemetery sleep hundreds of

★ Corfiot for a leg glide.

sailors and soldiers of the squadrons and regiments stationed in Corfu between 1814 and 1864, mostly killed by disease, and mostly young; servants of the civil administration; wives and children, only too often tiny babies; seamen and other visitors from later years; expatriates who made their last homes here and desired no other resting-place; and together in one plot, the victims of the Albanian mines. There are not many to bring flowers to these graves, but all are tended with affection by George Psailas, the Maltese superintendent, who, like his father before him, knows them all as his children by name and has now been awarded the BEM.

(In 1949, one hidden reminder of the British presence lingered in the weights and measures still in use. In the rest of Greece, goods were weighed by the Turkish *oka* (c. 2¾ lb.), which was divided into 400 *dramia*, or drams; in Corfu the measures were the *litra*, or pound, and the *ongia*, or ounce. Liquids were sold by the *kartoutso* (quart) and the *pinta* (pint), while you could buy a length of anything by the *intsa* or the *yarda*. Now the dull practicality of the decimal system rules, and these grains of the spice of life have gone the way of the guinea, the half-crown and the farthing.)

Nightfall brought animation to the heart of the town. It was the hour of the *corso*, the promenade. All the tables of the Liston cafés were crowded, under both the arcade and the Plateia trees. The broad pedestrian way between was filled with citizens, passing slowly and re-passing in either direction – couples, both young and old, whole families with children down to babies in prams, groups of girls with linked arms, bright as butterflies in summer dresses, laughing and talking among themselves and pretending not to be trying to catch the appraising eyes of the prowling packs of boys. They were, almost without exception, decent, well-behaved children of strict families, which made the underlying excitement all the keener.

After an ouzo, sipped at the same leisurely pace as the

meandering crowds, we would go a little way out of town and eat in the open at Vasili's restaurant, where the service was so slow that even the Corfiots noticed it and gave the place the nickname '*Ypomoni*', which means Patience. Later, or very much later – depending on Vasili's whim – we walked the almost empty streets, putting off the moment when we must go to our segregated lodgings. Once we heard men's voices in song, which grew louder as we came down the street. We turned a corner to find a quartet with a guitar, serenading in close harmony an open window on the second floor above them. It was a traditional rite of courtship to hire such a band of musicians to declaim sentimental ballads beneath one's mistress's bedroom. The singers were not full-time professional musicians. On a visit to the butcher Marily found the shop unmanned, and was directed to the street corner where the shopkeeper was rehearsing with his colleagues for the night's vicarious wooing.

A bent for music seemed to pervade Corfu society at all levels. Until the war, touring opera companies from Italy had regularly sung Italian opera at the old theatre and much of their repertoire was familiar. When the film of *Rigoletto* was shown at the Phinika cinema, even the errand-boys went about whistling 'La donna e mobile'. On one occasion when Marily and I came out of the family town house, we heard music further along the street of the Saint and saw the bishop, with his chaplain, standing at the open door of a tavern. Inside, four or five workmen of rough appearance and doubtful sobriety were ending a song. When the *despotis* had thanked them, they offered to sing for him at diocesan headquarters. He made no promises, but gave them a benediction and left. We asked the men to sing for us and settled for Verdi. A short consultation followed and they were off in full blast on a chorus, *fortissimo* throughout, but word perfect and in faultless harmony.

Corfiot music had an Italian rather than a Greek flavour. This is much less evident today. The powerful recording industry is centred in Athens; inevitably what pours forth day and night from cassette players and juke-boxes is the music of the mainland and the Aegean world, dominated now by the bouzouki. The old *cantadhes*, sung to the guitar or mandolin, are hardly to be heard above the din. But then, when the peak of reproduction was the 78 rpm gramophone record, there was more time and taste for live performance. It was not uncommon, in a taverna or restaurant, for one or two customers to break into gentle, melodious song, for their own pleasure and that of the other eaters. Even the church music of the Ionian, in both melody and harmony, is less alien to West European ears than the harsh Near Eastern cadences of the Byzantine chant as it is sung in Athens.

One thing which has not changed is the sound of the island's brass bands – the Old Philharmoniki and the Man-tzaro of the town (the latter named after the composer of the National Anthem) and their humbler relations from villages such as Gastouri, Skripero and Synaradhes. Each has its novices and trainees, ambitious to be selected in the full band as it marches, glorious in piped blue uniforms and brazen plumed helmets, in the Litanies of the Saint. The peculiar lunch-time noise of Corfu is the cacophony of earnest clar-inettists, trumpeters and tuba players, each one practising his own part, in the Philharmonic Society's upper room.

Eight

Because Marily was staying with her mother, brothers and sister, at the house on the Spianada, it was natural that I should spend most of my time there. It was a reunion of a sort, for I had known them all in Athens in 1945, when the twins were boys of thirteen and Elisabeth a small round six-year-old. Now the two brothers were tall young men and as different in looks and temperament as any twins could be. Nicky was outstandingly handsome, touchy and proud and very conscious of family tradition; Stevie's friendly bespectacled face reflected a more easygoing and democratic temperament. Elisabeth was about to be a pretty bridesmaid.

The other members of the household were Angeliki the maid ('Jellicoe' to us), a middle-aged Corfiot who, as was common among Greek house servants, was not at all shy in contributing to family discussions; and the dog, Koko. Koko was a wire-haired fox terrier with an independence of character bordering on eccentricity and the only dog I have ever heard of to develop an amorous attachment for a pig. His official name was 'English'. As a puppy he had belonged to an officer in the British Forces which came to Greece in 1941. His master had to leave Athens in the face of the German invasion and found a home for the pup with Marily's family. They christened him 'English' so as to have an excuse for annoying the Germans by calling loudly to him in the street.

The ménage was dominated by the ebullient personality of my mother-in-law-to-be. She was a big lady, in every respect, and her powerful voice of summons and command penetrated continually to the furthest corners of the house. Generous, impatient, capable of sudden anger but never of bearing a grudge, possessively caring of her children, loyal to her many friends and to all who worked for her, interested in every aspect of the human race, fluent in English, French and German as well as her native Greek, a voracious reader, particularly of English fiction, she had a vast zest for life. She was at the time fancy-free, after the collapse of her second marriage, and still possessed of the sense of mischief which had established her reputation, as a girl, as the *enfant terrible* of Athenian society. We all laughed a great deal.

The atmosphere of the Bulgari family circle was so different that it was easy to understand that her first marriage had stood a slender chance of success. It took me much longer to appreciate them, partly because they were different from any kind of family that I had ever known and partly because we communicated less easily. But the love which had existed between Marily and her grandfather, from her childhood, helped to open the door for me. Nono – the Corfiots use the Italian word for grandpa, rather than the Greek *pappous* – was actually one year younger than my parents, Marily being the product of the early marriage and I of a late one. I thought of him as older, however, no doubt for psychological reasons. He was a small man, his keen handsome face adorned with the beard of an Orthodox priest, not long and bushy like most, but pure white and neatly trimmed. He also wore his white hair short. One suspects that the Bulgari priests used their unique position in the ecclesiastical structure to dispense themselves from some of the stricter canons of outward appearance. Papa Stephano's father (he who ended his days in Nice) when travelling abroad used to embark dressed as a priest and at once changed, in his cabin, into civilian clothes. Priests are reputed to be Jonahs on a sea voyage and he was not surprised, on one trip, to hear a fellow passenger ask what had become of that 'filthy *papas* who came aboard with us'.

Papa Stephano was a cultivated man, who corresponded widely on literary and artistic topics. In his later years, when he was free from battling with the Church authorities and the burden of administering the saint's affairs, he took up again with his first love and painted prolifically. Many of his pictures survive – landscapes, country scenes and portraits – nearly all in oils. They vary in quality, but the best display a considerable talent; the style is oddly old-fashioned, probably because of the long gap of years when he was prevented from developing his art. He died the year after our marriage. It is my regret that I never had the chance to discuss with him his philosophy of life. My guess is that he was a devout sceptic whose doubts were not strong enough to overcome the pull of the divine fishing-line. He was certainly a good man, who did his duty and more in the service of the saint, and never lost a lightness of heart which enabled him to come to terms with disappointment.

His wife Maria, Marily's Nona, was a contrast. She had been a beauty in her youth and was still a very handsome old lady, with hair which had been snow-white since she was thirty, an erect carriage and a majestic bust. She was stately in movement, full of gracious words and given to composing flowery prose effusions, heavy with the pathetic fallacy. I found her less sympathetic than her husband, and difficult to relate to. She had, however, suffered the loss of an only daughter and she was a good wife to the priest in all their vicissitudes.

Maria's mother had been Italian, from Turin, and her father of the old Corfu family of Giallina, who owned considerable estates in the island. (One of her uncles was Angelo Giallina, the painter, whose landscapes capture with remarkable truth the dream-like quality of Corfu's atmosphere.) She was the eldest of three sisters. The second, Silvia, had been married at one time to a sea-captain of the Lloyd Triestino line, named Ilario, whom she sometimes accompanied on his voyages. Unfortunately, some time before the war when Ilario was on leave and staying with the Bulgari family in Corfu, he decided that he had enough and departed in circumstances of high drama – surreptitious packing of suitcases, note left on mantelpiece, frantic pursuit to the port, confrontation, hysterics – which have become legendary in the telling. He never came back and Silvia made her home, for the remaining forty-five years of her life, first with her older sister and then with her nephew Spiro, Marily's father.

She, too, must have been a lovely girl, but she had not worn so well as Maria, and was, when I first knew her, already becoming reclusive and a little odd. Her letters were almost impossible to read, being written in Greek transliterated into Roman script, in a spidery sloping hand, and complicated by her old-fashioned paper-saving trick of writing twice over on the same side of the sheet, the second time at right angles to the first.

Aunt Lydia, the third sister, had also made a childless marriage which ended in divorce. She lived alone on a family property at the village of Viro, a thin, ill-looking, unhappy woman who, it was said, drank too much. Bits of the property had been sold, little by little, to pay debts and she was left with the small, charming, but decrepit house, a tangle of gardens and a grove of trees producing the finest oranges in the world.

There was a whiff of defeat in the air and none of the family felt the departure of ancestral glory more sharply than Marily's father, Spiro Bulgari. He had an almost incestuous affection for his native island, so strong that he never, if he could help it, set foot outside it, even to the mainland opposite. But it was more truly a nostalgia for the Corfu of the Venetians, and for the aristocratic principle. Since the end of the *Enetokratia* everything had been gradually going downhill. The British had, for a while, stopped the rot, confirming the old families in their privileges and even making some of their members Knights of the Most Noble Order of St Michael and St George. But the Greeks of the modern state seemed to him irredeemably vulgar. 'Ach! Romyi,'* he

* viz. Romans (Romaioi). The citizens of the Byzantine, or East Roman, Empire so

would say wearily, contemplating a party of Athenians with brown and white co-respondents' shoes and too much jewellery, asserting themselves in the overbearing accents of the capital.

He was not much more polite about the ordinary people of the island. A race *'senza fede'* he described them – without faith, not to be trusted. And indeed the Corfiots had a traditional reputation for treachery and the stiletto. They certainly tend to use charm as a substitute for reliability. 'We are all terrible liars, you know,' they say with a disarming smile and offer you a drink, or a basket of mulberries, to compensate for having let you down for the third time. One might almost be in the Outer Hebrides, except for the weather.

I may be making my father-in-law sound like a sour and snobbish *fainéant*, but in fact his nature was at odds with his attitudes. He was, when I first knew him, an active and highly intelligent man of forty-three – though not as intellectually inclined as his father. He held for many years the post of administrative director of the Corfu Psychiatreion, which he ran so well that it had the reputation of being one of the best in Greece. This was not simply a tribute to his efficiency. He showed a genuine affection for the unfortunates under his care and generated a spirit of calm and goodwill which made up for the hospital's shortcomings in modern facilities.

The old madhouse still stands where it did, beside the main road that runs southward out of town from Sarocco Square. A garden with high railings adjoins the road, under whose eucalyptus treees the less disturbed residents shamble about for most of the day, occasionally begging a cigarette or a drachma from passers-by. This can only be therapeutic for those outside as well as in. One defective called Taso was well known to the community, because he was allowed to

---

designated themselves, and the name continued to be applied to the Greeks under Ottoman occupation. In the mouth of a Corfiot, with all the advantages of the superior Venetian occupation, it was a term of disrespect.

carry a banner in the saint's processions. These outings, four times a year, were all that Taso lived for. Clad in a voluminous blue cassock, he lumbered, splay-footed, bearing aloft the banner of the Panayia on an enormous pole and exchanging grins and garbled greetings with friends in the crowd. His sense of location being poor, he sometimes wandered from his proper place in the procession, causing disruption in the ranks of brass bands and cohorts of marching high school girls; but any threat to bar him from taking part so upset Taso that the Director preferred to risk official displeasure rather than the suicide of one of his patients.

Spiro was easy and popular in all types of company; loved women, particularly pretty ones, whom he charmed with his beautiful manners and melancholy good looks; played excellent bridge; had a deep knowledge of the history and society of Corfu; and was an accomplished cook. His second marriage was to Katie Palatianou, one of whose antecedents first deceived her husband with, and subsequently married, Sir Frederick Adam, the Lord High Commissioner after Maitland. Spiro had the rare distinction of celebrating his golden wedding with his second wife.

The heartland of the clan was the old house next to the church. Some parts of the structure date from the time when the church itself was built, in the late sixteenth century. Altered, enlarged and reconstructed, it has been the home of the Bulgaris ever since. Most of the dignified high houses of old Corfu, like the soaring 'lands' of the Old Town of Edinburgh, are tenements, designed as such from the outset, of individual flats at each level, opening off a common stair. Very few are, like this one, a complete self-contained dwelling-house.

The street door gave on to a passageway, leading at the rear to a small office, a servant's bedroom and the dark doorway into the back of the church. On the right lay Maro's territory, the kitchen, with its charcoal-burning cooking stove, olive oil store and an ice-box, regularly replenished in the hot weather with a half *colonna* from the ice-monger's hand-cart. Maro was a tiny village woman from Gastouri and was in service with the family for almost all her long life. At this time she must have been in her fifties, but her round simple face was so wrinkled that she appeared, to me at least, much older. With her kerchief, her long petticoats and skirts and shuffling walk, she resembled a Mediterranean Mrs Tiggy Winkle.

A narrow wooden stair, dimly lit by a curious Gothic window, with panes of various colours, led to the first floor. Most of the activity of the house went on here. It comprised a plainly furnished parlour, with windows commanding the whole of the street, Nono and Nona's spacious bedroom, Nono's study, and a bathroom. There was also an anomalous room, obtruding into the structure of the church, where Aunt Silvia lived her secret life and jealously guarded her privacy and store of personal treasures. Once a year it became a unique manufactory. It is possible to arrange for the saint's casket to be opened and to pay him special veneration by kissing his feet, which are shod in embroidered slippers. These are renewed yearly. Aunt Silvia's contribution to hagiolatry was to cut up the discarded pair into very small scraps, each of which was then incorporated into an amulet, for sale to those of simple faith.

The second storey was taken up by the dining-room, with its hatch and lift for pulling food up from the kitchen; and the big *saloni*, used only for formal entertaining. On the top floor was Papa Stephano's studio, and a couple of small bedrooms. Marily and I occupied one of these for a few nights a little while after we were married, before starting our journey to Scotland. It was not a restful room. The bells of the Saint rang for the first time at five o'clock and sounded – almost as it seemed just outside our window – at irregular intervals from then on. I used to get out of bed and watch from the window the steady trickle of townsfolk on their way to work who would not pass the church door without popping in to say good morning to their saint, sometimes leaving a barrow or other gear in the street outside.

The house gave no impression of opulence or conspicuous spending. The furniture was mostly nineteenth-century French and Italian work, of good but not exceptional quality, the pictures religious paintings or engravings of classical subjects, the books calf-bound sets of the works of authors such as Racine, Voltaire and Tasso. (The most noticeably English piece was an engraved reproduction of Frith's *Railway Station*.) Papa Stephano always did the family marketing, and was a well-known figure in the Piazza, going from shop to shop in his priest's robes and hat with a small boy behind him, hired for a drachma or two to carry the shopping baskets. At home he always wore the raso, varying from sturdy black to lightweight grey, according to the weather. Nona was never other than immaculately, even majestically, turned out. She supervised the kitchen activities, but did not cook, except occasionally to make a cake. A fair proportion of the day seemed to be spent in conversation with casual callers, fellow members in the main of the *ancien régime*, who have left in my memory a picture – probably much exaggerated – of innumerable little old ladies in black, wearing straw hats of the same colour. Strikingly, the talk was nearly always in Italian, which the Bulgaris, like other families of the same background, spoke among themselves in preference to Greek and with equal fluency (With the passing of the Victorian generation, this habit too has passed.)

Our marriage was preceded, a few days before the ceremony, by a rite which, preserved like a fly in amber, typified both the artificial etiquette of old Corfiot society and also its reluctance to move with the times. Marily, her mother and I went round the town late one afternoon, dropping visiting cards on as many as possible of those who had already been invited to the wedding. We engaged Francesco, the Maltese*

* The existence of a Maltese community in Corfu dates from the early years of the

cabman whom we generally used, to drive us from house to house in his carozza. At each stop he got down and handed in the cards while the three of us continued to sit at stately ease in the roadway.

As was common Greek practice, the majority of friends were invited only to the church. The reception was for the very close and for relatives. The other Aunt Lydia came, with her English husband, Charlie Blakeney, and their cool, soignée daughter Muriel. Lydia was Papa Stephano's sister and having married the British consul in Belgrade now lived with him, in his retirement, on a property on the mainland not far from Preveza. From Athens came Marily's mother's sister, Loukia, big and gruff but kind of heart and like a friendly boxer dog to look at. Her joy in life was to drive motor cars very fast. She was, in fact, an excellent amateur rally competitor.

Best of all, Marily's favourite grandmother, her Yiayia, Marika Pappou, with whom Ian and I had stayed in Athens. She was small and brisk, with faded red-gold hair and ate faster than anyone I have ever met. She was funny and intelligent and liked risqué jokes and was absolutely without hypocrisy or side. Only, in repose, her eyes showed a trace of the melancholy which was to darken her last years. She had memories of grand days. Her father, Dimitri Ralli, was prime minister when the Corinth Canal was inaugurated and took his daughter of thirteen with him on the first ship to sail through it. Marika accompanied him, too – during another premiership – on an official visit to the Turkish government at Constantinople. She received from Sultan Abdul Hamid – 'Abdul the Damned' – a piece containing so many diamonds

---

British Protectorate. Maltese stone was used for the building of the Palace of St Michael and St George, at the end of the Esplanade, and workmen were imported from Malta at the same time. Many of these settled in the town. Although now virtually integrated into Greek society, some families still have Maltese names and most remain loyal to the Roman Catholic faith. They have their cathedral and an agreeable bishop, easily distinguishable in the street by his habit of wearing a homburg hat with his soutane.

and emeralds that it had to be divided into two large brooches before it could decently be worn.

No photographic record of the wedding or the reception exists, except one blurred snapshot of the happy pair, in kilt and white bridal dress, walking from the Saint. The leading town photographer of the time, Mr Peroulis, was engaged, but put us all in stilted poses of such awfulness that my father-in-law with an imperious Bulgari gesture refused to order a single print, and that was that.

The first stage of the brand-new joint life-journey was made by taxi and took us seven miles out of town. Our destination was the house of San Stefano, which Lily Manessi, out of the warmth of her family friendship, had offered to us for the first week of our marriage. Spiro Botsi, Gastouriot and most-favoured *taxidzis* (like his son Costaki after him), drove us through the dark, taking us up to his village, to be shown off and to buy a bottle of ouzo, and then past the empty Achillion, down the steep zig-zags to the sea and finally up again, along the cypress-lined drive to the old house on its rock.

Today the most conspicuous landmark for anyone sailing past the east coast of the island is the white bulk of the San Stefano Hotel, conflicting starkly with the curves of the landscape. Much of the estate has also been sold as building plots. Then, however, it was whole, as it had been for many generations, with just the house set in its citrus grove and gardens and the acres of olive and cypress. The original house of the Flambouriari family, to which Lily belonged, had stood a little to the south; a small monastery occupied the present site and gave the whole property its name. The monks' cells became the stables of the second house, which still has a little church on the level below, as a private chapel.

The next morning I stepped for the first time on to the long balcony with its stone parapet, curving gently like the deck of a ship, which I was to know so well in the years to come. A rock face fell sheer to the courtyard of the church, and behind the plain metal cross and pierced stone tracery of the *kambanario* and its bells stretched the expanse of the gulf. The water was like silk and a golden pathway of sun dwindled into the mist hiding the far mountains.

It was a comfortable house for two lovers, not large, and homely with its floors of scrubbed wood and white-painted cedar ceilings. Artemisia and Georgina, lent to us with the house, looked after us discreetly and affectionately. In the morning we used to walk down through the woods and swim from a narrow, pebbly beach and toil back in the fierce midday heat. At sunset the *gri-gri* boats came wheeling out from the little harbour of Benitses for the night's fishing – a motor caique towing the *mana* with the nets and behind it three small boats with carbide lamps, like a duck with her brood of ducklings. After dark their lights lay on the water far out in the gulf, while nightly the prying moon grew larger in the sky. The only night sounds were the occasional bark of a distant dog and the monotonous fluted note of the *ghioni,* the small scops owl.

By the time we left San Stefano, the grandparents had moved their establishment to the country house at Gastouri and we went to stay there. For me this was to peel another skin from the onion of experience. For Marily it involved the stirring of complicated memories. She had spent so many summer holidays at Gastouri, first as a young child with her father and mother, and after their divorce with her small brothers, coming from Athens to Corfu when the long school holidays began. The move up from town followed a regular pattern. The luggage was loaded on a long low cart – a *lissa* – and went ahead with pale Andriana the housemaid and Efthalia, the wall-eyed and bad-tempered cook. A car conveyed Marily's governess, Miss Godfrey, and the twins and their English nanny. Last travelled a carozza holding Nono, Nona and Marily. The five-mile journey took nearly an hour, for it was a steep pull up the long hill from Pondis's taverna, often requiring the passengers to dismount and walk behind. On arrival, everyone ate a picnic lunch of salami, pickled cucumber and Edam cheese.

The house is at the very edge of the village. It always seemed to be full of people. Thodhori, the factor, and his wife, Tasia, lived in a cottage which formed part of the outbuildings. Maro and a servant named Vaso helped in the kitchen. Various men and women of the village did part-time work in the garden, and in the vineyards and olive and almond groves below the village which belonged to the estate; they would drop in to discuss country matters and settle accounts with Papa Stephano. (Some of the younger women, such as Lefko and Marigoula, were great beauties, maintaining the village's reputation for producing lovely brides.) Local children – suitably approved – came to play with Marily in the garden, bringing their dolls or marbles. There were also the inevitable social visits, as well as formal dinner parties.

So the long hot days and weeks passed, spent almost wholly among the summer sounds and scents of the garden. Expeditions to the seaside were rare, needing much organisation. Marily missed her mother and recalls listening for the sound of the car climbing the hill which would bring one of her visits. Miss Godfrey, tall, jolly and golden-haired, was a consoling companion, but the one abiding compensation was the affection which grew between her and her grandfather. He took her side against petticoat government, shared private jokes with her and showed his love in the portraits which he painted.

Stan Stefano stands on the open hillside for all to see. Gastouri is a hidden house, invisible until you climb an oblique stair beside the garden wall and turn in at the gate. In this it is more typical of Corfu, where habitations, whether villages or houses, tend to huddle on the slopes away from the sea. Thucydides mentioned, as a sign of the political stability created by civilisation, the shift of population from the hills to the sea-coast, once the fear of pirates was removed. The siting of the hundred or more villages of Corfu illustrates the reversal of this process during the Middle Ages. Maps of the nineteenth century show that even then the main road to the south was not the present one by the coast and Benitses, but headed inland, climbing to Ayious Deka and Stavro, before descending the valley of the Mesonghi river to the narrow tail of the island.

The gate opened into a front garden of formal beds and gravel paths, separated by low box hedges. On the right stood a tall, flourishing Canary palm, a common sight outside the grander houses of Corfu, where they were planted more as a status symbol than for the fruit, which does not ripen so far north. A path ran straight ahead to the foot of a flight of stone steps. These led to a small semicircular terrace, with a double door and french window, in the centre of the west front of the low house. The ground behind was planted with a thick grove of bay trees, giving protection from village dwellings on the slope above, and shade to a circular clearing equipped with benches, tables and garden chairs. An area of about half an acre to the left of the house contained lemon and almond trees, a large walnut tree, some haphazard beds of vegetables and two pergolas of vines bearing table grapes – muscat, Isabella and rosaki. There was also a large underground cistern filled with rain water from the roof. (During our stay we had one of the majestic thunderstorms which are a Corfu speciality, in the course of which, with a noise like the end of the world, lightning struck the concrete cover of the cistern and cracked it from end to end.)

The terrace door opened directly into the main public room, a large *saloni* with a wooden floor and ceiling, furnished with a variety of chairs and sofas, an outsize, but totally unplayable, grand piano, a tiger-skin rug of obvious antiquity and, in the centre, a large round table, on which reposed at all times a bound volume of all fifty-two numbers of the *Illustrated London News* of 1904. (There being virtually no other reading matter in the house, this afforded a unique opportunity of following the fortunes of the Russo-Japanese war.) Opposite the main entrance, another double window and door led to the bay-tree garden, the room thus filling the whole width of the house. One corner was occupied by a His Master's Voice gramophone, wound up by hand for each record and amplifying the sound by means of a horn of remarkable size. The collection ranged from rag-time tunes of the twenties, through popular arias and choruses from Italian opera, to half a dozen primordial one-sided discs, of double thickness, on which the voice of Caruso had been tinnily captured.

Above the cavernous fireplace at one end of the room, a gilt-framed mirror displayed a long, irregular crack, which remains to this day as a souvenir of the British Army. In the wake of the German withdrawal in 1944 an infantry unit occupied the house as the mess for its officers, one of whom, elevated by the heady atmosphere of liberation, shied a full inkpot at the mirror. The stain on the marble mantel echoed the one on the stele which I had seen in the Acropolis museum.

Opposite the hearth, the *saloni* extended through an open archway into a small dining-room and beyond that lay the kitchen. This had the air of a medieval outhouse, with a rough flagged floor and a roof of bare beams and rafters sloping down to the farther wall. An array of much-worn copper pans and dishes hung above an antiquated cooking stove, fired only by charcoal. There was one deep stone sink and the water for this was stored in big earthenware pots. Water was heated on a stove, burning wood and charcoal, with a metal oven attached to it, and there was also a brick oven for the baking of bread.

The house had no piped water at that time. Clothes were washed in cold rain-water at the cistern and once a month there was a *bougadha*, or washing of household linen, which could take up to three days to complete. In this, after an initial wash, the linen was folded and piled in layers in a wicker basket. Muslin, wrapped round wood ash and rosemary, was laid on top and boiling water poured through it. No other method makes such white sheets. The water for drinking and cooking was carried by women from the spring. To fetch it they had to walk about half a mile, passing down through the village, past the baker's *fourno*, over the bridge across the ravine and up again towards the lower half of the village, locally called Pahatika. Half way there, an immense plane tree stands beside the road. A companion, of even greater girth, grows a few yards up the hillside; the hollow space inside the trunk is the size of a small cell and was used as such by a poor dotty old woman when Marily was a child.

A perennial spring has always gushed from the hillside close to the planes and provided Gastouri with a constant supply of sweet pure water. The Empress Elisabeth, when she was using the Achillion as her retreat, had the spring piped into a little domed reservoir, with an inscription proclaiming it to be the 'Spring of the Empress Elisabeth', but the village calls the place simply the Platanos – the Plane Tree. Here, in the evening, women and girls from all the households used to foregather with jars and four-gallon cans, and exchange the gossip of the day while awaiting their turn at the taps and then in twos and threes sway gracefully homewards, never spilling a drop from the load miraculously balanced on their heads.

The sleeping quarters of the house lay at the opposite end from the kitchen. A door of the *saloni* led directly to a bedroom which Marily and I used and in turn the grandparents' room opened from ours without an intervening passage. The same applied to the third bedroom, which had been Marily's in the old days. Coming out of the other door of that room, back towards the *saloni*, one entered a passageway giving access to a lavatory so small that there was just space for a human being between the door and the pan.

(Needless to say, this had no cistern but was flushed from a pail.) The passage itself was used, on occasions of state or compelling necessity, for the ceremony of the bath. A round tin tub was brought and filled with water, heated on the kitchen stove. In this the bather soaped himself or herself, while an appropriate attendant poured water from jugs.

The final completion of the circuit back to the *saloni* was by way of something between a bedroom and a corridor, used, as by some Chekovian poor relation, by Aunt Silvia. Since it was the shortest route to the lavatory, and Silvia objected to her domain being used for transit, much time and ingenuity was wasted on stratagems to deprive her of her keys and prevent her from barring the access.

Not that time was in any sense a wastable commodity at Gastouri. There was too much of it, the hot airless time of summer, drowsy with the scent of the lemon and bay trees, in which it was easy to imagine that nothing much had ever happened there, or was ever likely to happen. Such a mixture of the elegant and the primitive, the combination of the unprudish intimacy of our domestic arrangements with the daily formality of a three-course luncheon, the semi-feudal contrast between, on the one hand, Nono in his neat white beard and black raso and Maria, always beautifully dressed, and, on the other, the diversity of rural characters coming and going in the house and garden, discussing matters of business, or the household, or their families, with a merry familiarity, yet always observing the conventional courtesies governing relations between the village and the big house – all this, set in the days' languid rhythm, kept not only Aunt Silvia but all of us, it seemed, trapped in a never-ending Chekhov play.

We had to be in town, of course, on 11 August for the saint's procession. There I saw for the first time the cassocked acolytes – including daft Taso – with gilded lanterns and vast banners; the bands of the town and of Gastouri and the other villages; the high school boys and girls, solemn in uniform dark blue, with white gloves, trying to slow-march – 'Ena-dyo. One-two' – in approximate time to two competing bands; contingents of Boy Scouts, Girl Guides, Sea Scouts; the twin polychrome files of priests, gold, green, blue, white and crimson, chanting into the flames of their candles; then the *despotis,* irascible old Bishop Methodius – no friend of the Bulgaris – with his flaring beard of cotton-wool; and last, flanked by a naval guard of honour with fixed bayonets and borne in his travelling casket by four priests, Spyridion's dark weary face, leaning towards one shoulder, while the crowd on either side rippled with the sign of the cross, made with the quick, triple Orthodox gesture.

I also saw, for the first and last time in his accustomed, ancestral position behind the saint he had served for so many years, the silver head of Papa Stephano. Within a few weeks we were on our way to a new life in Scotland, and before the next August Litania Nono was dead.

Nine

Over the next ten years we did not go to Greece more than half a dozen times, and that only on holiday for a month or so. Our three children were born, and it was more complicated than it is now to transport a young family back and forth across Europe. Our life in Scotland kept us busy enough. I was trying to build up a practice at the bar, and Marily to establish a warm and loving family home, where our friends would always find a welcome. Being what she is, she made many, and never met the reputed chilliness of Edinburgh folk towards incomers. She loved the steep windy streets and bold prospects of my native city, and endured, with only one or two murmurs, its fickle weather and barbaric drinking habits, and the lingering Scottish sabbatarianism which held that to enjoy oneself on Sunday was sinful or, worse, Mediterranean. Marily also came to share my special affection for the birch and pine woods and small lochs of the Forest of Rothiemurchus, and the peat-brown streams hurrying over the boulders between heather banks, from the distant Cairngorms. It was a happy time.

Even from a distance I came to know Greece as my second country by marrying into it, less romantically perhaps, but in a realistic and matter-of-fact way. As with relatives, I had no choice but to take the rough with the smooth. And what was going on in Greece during those years was often rough. The end of the civil war brought little stability and left much bitterness. The royal family, which could have acted as a symbol of national unity, became increasingly identified with the richer and more reactionary elements of society and lost its popularity. British influence in Greece had declined to invisibility, and the British government began to be seen as an enemy, because of the Cyprus question.

This was a matter which united Greeks of all political colours. The idea of *Enosis* – of union between Greece and Cyprus – was nothing new. It had been mooted, off and on, by successive Greek administrations ever since 1878, when Britain first occupied the island under an arrangement with the Ottoman Porte. To the Greeks it seemed to be demanded both by historical logic and by simple justice. Cyprus had been Greek in language and culture since the dawn of history. The Turks, who captured it from the Venetians only in 1571, were, from a Greek point of view, nothing but a bunch of upstart interlopers from Central Asia, of alien tongue and hostile faith. Those Turks who had settled on the island over the past three hundred years amounted to only about one fifth of its population. The modern kingdom of the Hellenes was the sole heir to, and representative of, the age-old Greek dominance of the eastern Mediterranean. If both Greeks and Cypriots wanted to be united, what justification was there for keeping them apart? Nor was the argument affected – if anything it was strengthened – by the fact that Britain, in 1925, had made Cyprus one of its Crown Colonies, without reference to the wishes of the people of either land.

Earlier appeals to the British government had met with a consistently negative response, but the issue did not acquire serious proportions until the early 1950s. The Greek government, under the premiership of Field-Marshal Papagos, made several approaches to the British government, which refused even to discuss the possibility of *Enosis*. In fact, *Enosis* had very litle practical chance of succeeding. It was anathema to Turkey, and would almost certainly have provoked a military invasion of the kind which eventually took place in 1974. But the government in London (with the bland tactlessness so familiar to the Scots) appeared to ignore even the existence of Greek aspirations, and implied that the Cypriots were silly foreigners who did not realise how well off they were under the kindly guidance of the Colonial Office.

Papagos took the matter to the United Nations, but got

little satisfaction. The result was the formation in 1955 of the National Organisation of Cypriot Combatants (EOKA), led by Colonel George Grivas, a fanatical Cypriot-born Greek officer, which embarked on a campaign of demonstrations and bombing attacks on property throughout the island. There quickly arose a state of disorder, not unlike the familiar Northern Irish scene, in which EOKA were regarded by one side as heroic soldiers for freedom and by the other as bloody terrorists. Predictably, the British government appointed a field-marshal as governor of the island, deported the effective leader of the Greek Cypriot community, Archbishop Makarios, to the Seychelles, and increased the number of troops in the garrison. As is usual in such situations, the army and police were forced to take retaliatory action, some of which was unnecessarily oppressive, and turned even well-disposed Cypriots into foes. Five years of bloodshed were to pass before a solution of some sort was devised, with the creation of an independent Cypriot republic, in which power was shared between the Greek and Turkish communities, and Britain, Greece and Turkey were all given the right to station troops on the island.

Throughout these unhappy years, popular sympathy in Greece was for *Enosis* and EOKA, and against Britain, which was seen – perhaps correctly – as being interested in Cyprus only as a base from which to protect the lines of communication of a now imaginary empire. The government in Athens championed the EOKA cause vociferously and poured out a stream of often venomous propaganda against Britain. The Greek press seized on every instance of British military or police behaviour which could be interpreted as brutality, torture or murder. In Corfu, Ionian Bank Square was renamed the Square of the Heroes of the Cypriot Struggle – and continued, of course, to be known as Theotoki Square, as it had been since the erection there of a statue of the statesman George Theotokis.

These international tensions provided both of us with a

useful exercise in respecting the other's point of view. When in Greece, I tried to maintain a dignified impartiality. It is fair to say that I was never treated offensively, or even impolitely, on account of my nationality. The waiter at a Psychiko *kafeneion* did once show signs of wanting to pick a quarrel with me, but the proprietor told him to be quiet, 'because I was married to a nice girl whose mother lives up the road'. Behind the strident chauvinism of the politicians and journalists one could see the flame of patriotism, and the pride in being Greek, burning as clearly as it had done in the days of the Italian war, and the hearts were as good as ever.

On our holidays we spent as much time in Athens as in Corfu. We had no house of our own on the island, and it was difficult to find anywhere suitable to stay. Indeed at that time I did not much like Corfu. In part this was due to the fact that I never felt well there. Something – I suspect the water, which used to bring our children up in large itchy bumps – gave me indigestion and general lassitude. More seriously, the island disturbed my spirit. It was almost too beautiful, with a softness of outline and atmosphere which had nothing to do with the Greece that I thought of as Greece. Among the everlasting olive trees I felt a nostalgia for the small pines exploding from the harsh red soil of Attica like bright green shell-bursts, and the light-loaded *meltemi* tossing the feathers of the pepper trees in the Athenian squares. Athens, too, was still little changed and unpolluted, with an easygoing small-town feel. We had many friends with whom to pass the warm evenings at open-air restaurants or cinemas.

From Athens we were able, by now, to make excursions to the nearer islands, such as Spetses and Aegina, or even, if Marily's mother could mind the children, further afield in the Aegean. One of these, coincidentally for me, was to Paros. Six of us decided to go there for a long weekend, on the strength of a rumour praising a new hotel, in a converted mill, at a place called Dhryos on the north-west coast of the island. Beside Marily and me, there were her brother Nicky, now married to his French wife Anne, and her brother and sister-in-law. We made the booking at an agency in Athens who gave us a confirmatory piece of paper, and the advice to travel from the port to Dhryos by taxi.

Voyaging to Paros had advanced in sophistication since the days of the *Ay. Nikolaos*, but not very far. We travelled on the SS *Myrtidhiotissa*, a handsome boat approaching the end of her useful life. (The age of the SS was then beginning to yield to that of the MV.) She appeared to generate steam on coal slack or oily waste, for our progress across the sparkling Aegean was signalled, like that of some latter-day Israelites, by a moving pillar of thick black smoke. The master was a big, pale, flabby man, the very antithesis of my old *capetanios*, who sported on the little finger of his right hand an inch-long nail, the badge of one who has risen above the drudgery and stigma of manual labour. (It can also be used for removing wax from the ears.) The *Myrtidhiotissa* was the only ship on which I have seen, attached to the wall of the saloon, a small receptacle bearing the words COMPLAINING BOX.

We made a leisurely way past the familiar line of islands – Kythnos, Seriphos, Siphnos – fumigating the summer sky as we went. Meals and refreshments were taken. A lottery was held, with an octopus as prize. Just before sunset three dolphins joined our company, and swam together abreast, immediately in front of the ship's stern. Every so often one would roll on its side and turn its knowing eye and wide grin up at the admirers at the rail. Finally, after dark, we slid into Paroikia harbour and tied up.

Vehicular traffic had reached Paros since 1945, but the handful of taxis were all hired by travellers bound for Naoussa, quite the wrong way for Dhryos. Helpful locals pointed out a bus which they said might suit us, so we hurried across the square with our grips and inquired of the driver. No, he said, the bus didn't really go as far as that, but since there were six of us and one other couple going to Dhryos, he would, for an extra half a crown a head, take us there. The bus filled up. When every seat was occupied, stools were placed along the length of the central aisle. The racks and roof were crammed to overflowing with cases, cardboard boxes, baskets of provisions, and assorted livestock. When it was impossible to load another article, we set off. The time was now about half past ten.

The bus ground and lurched its way up the roughly metalled road to Lefkes, and beyond it to the crest of the island. Half way up we ran into hill mist, out of which, at the frequent stops, dim figures with oil lanterns loomed to extract their loved ones from the bus's steaming and garlicky interior. At last we were the only passengers left. We bumped onwards downhill for a long time, and finally came to rest in pitch darkness and what appeared to be an uninhabited waste. 'We have arrived', the driver said, and, rolling up his jacket as a pillow, he lay down on the floor and went to sleep.

We would probably have stayed there on the bare hillside all night, had not someone with a torch come to meet the other couple from the bus. We followed them in single file, carrying our bags, down an uneven, narrow path. After a quarter of a mile the sound of the sea could be heard, and the outline of an unlit building was just visible against the moonless sky. We found a door which opened into a room and there fell over a wicker chair and a man asleep in it. He agreed to fetch the hotel owner. In due course another man, in pyjamas, appeared with a light and asked who we were. We explained. He had never heard of us. We produced our piece of paper. 'Ah!' he said, and went away with it, leaving us once more in total darkness. It was by now well after midnight. My companions were beginning to show symptoms of irritation, but I had had a premonition that something of this was going to happen, coupled with a calm certainty that all would turn out well in the end. (Impending total disaster, averted by Odyssean resource, is an essential ingredient in the Greek recipe for life.) The owner returned, now wearing

ordinary trousers with his pyjama jacket. Yes, he said grave-
ly, our booking was perfectly in order, except for the fact
that the agency had omitted to inform him of it, and all his
rooms were full. 'But never mind. George,' (this to the
unlucky man from the wicker chair) 'get six pairs of sheets,
two carafes of water and a lantern, and take the ladies and
gentlemen to the annexe.'

George did as he was bidden. The seven of us set off back
along the path to the bus, and then a further quarter of a mile
up the stony hillside till we came to a freshly completed
house without glass in its windows, and furnished with
absolutely nothing except three pairs of double bunks.
George spread the sheets, set down the lantern and the water
jugs, and before disappearing into the dark gave us a sweet
smile and said 'Good sleep and a good dawning.' We were
able to move into the hotel the next day. The food was good,
the swimming excellent, and everything moved on a time-
scale three hours behind the rest of the world. I think it no
longer exists.

We used to visit the Acropolis in Athens from time to time,
and I was able to explore it more thoroughly than when it
had been in the front line of battle. It was several years before
I saw Delphi. Four of us went there by car, leaving Athens in
the afternoon and arriving after dark. The moon was nearly
at the full and very brilliant as we drove down the long
gradient from Arachova, lighting quite clearly the wide river
of olive trees which fills the valley between Delphi and the
sea.

We had booked for the night at the Kastalia – at that time
one of the only two hotels in the village. After dinner we
walked down towards the Castalian spring. We were accompanied by an uncanny moaning, which seemed to have its
source in the site of ancient Delphi, high above us to our left.
Presumably it was a trick of the night wind in the Shining
Rocks – the cliffs which tower above the ruined remains –
but it sounded like the Pythia wailing for her lost oracle, and

set my scalp pricking. At the spring we found a narrow path, which led upwards from the road into a wood. We decided to climb it. It emerged at the edge of the classical site, and there, almost as distinct as day in the moon's milky light, Apollo's temple, the theatre and treasuries, and the whole slope of jumbled marbles lay, silent and deserted, spread out before us, and beyond them the dramatic plunge of the mountain-side.

So, by luck, I was permitted, so to speak, a private view of each of the two most famous remains of ancient Greece. The contrast between the sightings could hardly have been grea-ter: the one on a brilliant winter morning in the middle of a battle, the other by a pale summer midnight moon. Yet the two complemented each other, for the difference in circum-stances suited the difference of the subjects. The Parthenon is a creature of the day, a hymn to human triumph, the glori-fication of a city. Delphi is one of the shrines of the psyche, .breath-catchingly numinous, the very centre of the Hellenic identity, forever wheeling in the eye of Zeus' eagles as they circle above the shining cliffs.

In 1960 the balance of our Greek life swung decisively to Corfu, when we got the house at Mesonghi. I had been there once before, in the summer when we were married. Marily's father took us with him to visit the property, which is by the sea about twelve miles south of the town. We were driven in one of the venerable taxis, along the Perama corniche, past San Stefano, through Benitses and on to Moraitika. There the car left the road and took a meandering course through the middle of a large olive grove to the bank of a sluggish river, close to where it reached the sea. There were a few boats moored on the other side, below a half-ruined house, and a call brought forth a ferryman, who rowed us across.

The village struck me as the dirtiest I had seen in Corfu, and in the poorest repair. It consisted of two distinct groups of rather mean houses, separated by some two hundred yards of seashore. Between the halves of the village stood a square, two-storied house, with a long low building like a barn attached to it. The house also appeared to be in poor condition, and was occupied by a local village couple and their young son. They did so, however, as caretakers, for the house, together with the olive grove behind the beach, belonged to the Bulgari family. None of them, I was told, had lived there for many years, after a forebear of Marily's died there of malaria. The place was plagued by mosquitoes and was reputed to be extremely unhealthy.

To me, Mesonghi had a vaguely sinister air. The flat valley floor was covered with olive trees, as large as small oaks, hundreds of years old and looking as if they had been there since the beginning of time. Their huge trunks writhed in weird convolutions and had hollow bases, round which powerful roots seemed bonded into the ground like solidified lava. The beach was shingly and strewn with dead seaweed. Nothing stirred in the dingy village. It was very hot and still, and a heavy haze enclosed the bay. Cicadas sang relentlessly like the saws of tiny mad carpenters.

There was at that time no road to the village for mechanical transport, only a track along the right bank of the river from a mile or so upstream. However, when Marily went again with her father ten years later, a simple bridge – nothing more than a concrete plank, wide and strong enough for a lorry, and without any form of parapet – had been thrown across the river at its lowest narrow point, and it was possible to drive a car to the part of the village at the river's mouth. (To reach the other half, or the house, one had to find one's way through the olives.) The other important change was that, as part of the World Health Organisation's drive to eradicate malaria, the whole village had been liberally dosed with DDT and the anopheles mosquitoes had disappeared.

Seeing that the property was now both accessible and habitable, Marily looked at it with a new eye. She saw that the sea-bed of the bay, beyond the water's edge, consisted of

gently sloping sand, offering safe swimming for young children. The house and barn stood only twenty metres from the
water, and the shore could easily be cleared of seaweed. It is
also among the most beautiful places in Corfu, with the long
curve of bay between the river sand-bar and the rocky point
by the Kodhraka spring, the tall shapely hill of Chlomos, and
the gulf stretching eastwards to the shadowy outline of the
mainland.

Inspired, she asked her father to let her have the barn (more
accurately an *elaiotrivion,* or *litrouvio,* where the olives used to
be pressed for oil) for conversion into a summer holiday
house. Her father expressed doubts about the sanity of anyone wanting to live at the place whose climate had done for
Great-Uncle Victor, but she insisted, and he agreed to give
her the building, with the land down to the beach, and for
about thirty metres behind. So the Mesonghi years began.
Yanni and Eleni, the caretaking couple, were found other
accommodation in the village, and the *litrouvio* was emptied
of its assorted contents. One of these was an old millstone,
about six feet in diameter and eighteen inches thick, which
we set for a table in front of the house.

The plan of the house was very simple. In the centre was
the large living area, with the original doors opening, one
towards the sea, and the other to the olive grove. At one end
we made two bedrooms and a small bathroom, at the other a
room with double bunks for the children, the kitchen and
store-room, and an extra small bedroom and lavatory. The
floors were of sand-coloured brick, which needed only to be
swept clean, and the ceilings of long bamboos supported by
joists. This kept the house as cool as possible, and also
allowed one to hear what was said by anyone else anywhere
in the house. Most important of all for ease of living was the
construction of a verandah on the sea side, with whitewashed square columns and a slanting roof of bamboo and
bracken. Our nice stammering joiner – Spiro the Saw – made
the bunks and a plain table and two benches, and with a

couple of beds, a few pieces of family furniture, and some canvas chairs we were ready for the first summer's occupation.

Ten

Before us, there was only Mesonghi as it had always been. Now Mesonghi is a resort in the package holiday brochures, and, when you get there, an unplanned, graceless jumble of hotels, apartments, tavernas, cafés, discothèques, mini-markets and shacks selling souvenirs and sun-tan lotion. The beach is littered with umbrellas, sunbeds, pedalos, and bare breasts – mostly British – in an infinite range of proportions and allure. The villagers prosper, though not so greatly as their puppeteers, the London tour operators. The transitional summers were ours.

At the beginning the village had no electricity, and for several years we used only paraffin lamps and candles, becoming so fond of their mellow light that we were reluctant to change them for the convenience of turning on a switch. We did, of course, in the end, if only to escape the nuisance of replenishing the ice-box. A telephone we never got, and part of the spice of life was that all our visitors were unexpected, heralded only by the sound of a car horn or the rap of the brass dolphin doorknocker.

Mesonghi had no piped water and depended on a few wells and a fresh spring nearly half a mile up the hill. We had our own well on the property, not far from the house. The conversion had included the installation of a cistern in the roof space, from which the bathroom and kitchen taps drew water. It was supplied from the well by means of a hand-pump, and took about half an hour's manual labour to fill. This was usually done for a small fee by Spiro, the son of Niko and Maria, our nearest neighbours – known, to distinguish him from the joiner and various other Spiros, as Spiro the Pump. In the end we took pity on him and ourselves and fitted a small petrol-driven motor. The well water was considered fit only for washing; drinking water had to be fetched from the spring. As at Gastouri, it was carried by women on their heads, and was stored in porous pots for coolness.

After mules and donkeys, the Corfiot women were the commonest beasts of burden. They invariably balanced their loads on their heads, achieving the exact poise with amazing sureness, and using nothing but a little roll of cloth to protect their scalps from hard, heavy weights. They practised this skill from a very early age and developed an uprightness of carriage and a distinctive sinuous grace in walking which they kept all their lives. In the course of a single early morning drive into town, I have seen, in my headlights, a barefoot woman carrying on her head a bunch of zinnias to sell in the market, and, later, a labour force of girls, extending the Benitses harbour mole, each with a large stone on her head, graceful as a frieze of caryatids. Such sights are still to be seen, but are becoming less usual as modern sophistication modifies old village ways. (So ingrained was the habit that Maria, helping in our kitchen, was discovered with a frying-pan balanced on her head, not being able, she explained, to find anywhere to put it.)

Mesonghi seemed to me no longer sinister, but sad, like a village which had lost its heart. The standard of living was not far above bare subsistence. Some fields and gardens, worked mainly by women, a short distance up river, provided the basic necessities, supplemented by some fishing. But it was not a true fishing village, having no harbour and only boats small enough to be manoeuvred over the shallows into the shelter of the river. At evening one or two *paraghadhia* – long baited lines held at the surface by floats – would be laid, but the sandy waters of the bay were poor in fish, and the morning catch generally disappointing. Otherwise the men passed their days playing cards, with much slapping of winners on the table, in the *kafeneion* run by the village president, Mitso Rossi.* There was neither church nor school, and the houses and lanes were as dishevelled and untidy as I remembered them from 1949.

The people of Chlomos, high on the hill, professed to despise the Mesonghites as a do-less lot, and not real Corfiots anyway. No village could have survived in that situation in the heyday of piracy, and in fact Barbary corsairs habitually used the mouth of the river as a haven, and as a base for incursions inland. This continued until the French took Corfu from the Venetians and cleared the Ionian of pirates. The French governor, General Donzelot, encouraged settlement in the fertile, but undeveloped, river lands, and made public funds available for that purpose. The first villagers may well have been incomers from Epirus across the water. The Bulgari house dates from roughly the same period.

The villagers, proper Corfiots or not (we liked to think that their manners lacked the traditional island courtesy), reacted sullenly to our appearance on the local stage. The principal source of friction was the fact that the natural route between the two halves of the village passed between the house and the top of the beach, and a well-worn path cut across our land a few feet from the new verandah. When Marily took up residence for the first time, she tried to divert the pedestrian traffic a little further from the house by putting up two short and inconspicuous bamboo fences, running towards the sea on either side of her ground. In the morning the fences had disappeared. She had them replaced, and then asked one of our friends to spend the night at the house and keep watch. This he did, bringing a conspicuous shotgun with him. This achieved its object, but there was clearly a measure of ill-will, led, it was hinted, by one Aristides, a stout, rubicund man with fair hair and blue eyes and a brood

* (The price list on the wall began: OUZO 1 dr, KONIAK, 1 dr, CAFES 1 dr, TEA 2 dr, before passing on the luxury items such as gazoza and ouisky. The cloth-capped card players occasionally ordered a drink, but I never saw anyone actually pay for one.)

123

of blond, blue-eyed children. Marily decided that the best remedy was to invite the neighbours to a party. Relations with the village from then on were reasonably civil, and, as a gesture of goodwill, Aristides sent his wife round with a dish of rich, peppery eel *stifado* stew.

The matter of the right of way was never completely resolved. One of the café regulars, a dour elderly man, felt it his duty to maintain it, and did so by walking along the old path, usually when we had company and were drinking an evening ouzo round the millstone. With his cap pulled well down over his eyes, without a greeting, and looking neither to right nor left, he would weave his way between the chairs as if none of us existed.

The sea had brought us to Mesonghi, and it was the sea that drew the eye and soothed the spirit, from the moment when the sun leapt up from the peaks of Epirus and laid a golden blade on the water towards us. In early August, the mornings were dead calm, with no more than a ripple nuzzling the shore. Sometimes it was so hazy that a fisherman lifting his lines seemed to be suspended between heaven and earth in an element common to both.

We spent the mornings in and around the water. The gently shelving sand of the sea bottom made learning to swim easy and safe for the children. We also had constructed for us a little wooden jetty – what they call a *ponte* in Corfu – where we could sunbathe and watch the shoals of tiny fish, and the hermit crabs crawling over the sand, concealed by their movable shell homes. The jetty served as a mooring for the *Glaros* (Greek for seagull), our sturdy rowing-boat, the work of Costa the boat-builder at Benitses. Later, when the children were older, he built a canoe for them, which we kept on the beach.

Apart from local people passing along the shore, to and from the halves of the village, we had it and the sea to ourselves. Country folk at that time hardly bathed in the sea at all, and few of them could swim. The days of water-skiing, wind-surfing and such sports were still a long way off. In late August, the unsporting sport of *kefalo* fishing provided a diversion. The *kefalo*, or grey mullet, spawns at this time of year, and Mediterranean fishermen have taken advantage of this fact at least since Roman times (it is mentioned by the naturalist Pliny), and presumably long before that. A female – the *bafa* – is first caught, and then towed behind a boat in the shallows, by means of a line passed through her gills. Interested males crowd after her, and when two or three are busy in trying to attract her attention, the fisher slips out of the boat and deftly casts a circular net over them. The unfortunate living bait can be used over and over again. Our village expert, Spiro the Fish, was a pale, religious youth with a sly manner, who sang as a psaltis at the Benitses church. We did not care much for him, but he provided us with that best of Greek meals, fish taken straight from the sea and grilled, and eaten in the shade with a bottle of retsina and a view over blue water.

The bay took on a new charm in the late afternoon – the *vradhaki* – when the shadows of the house and olive trees began to creep down the beach. Swimming at that hour was, to my mind, less attractive, for the day's sun had warmed the water to the temperature of tepid soup. It was a time, rather, for talk and contemplation, while the colours shifted and faded on the gulf, the first stars appeared, the *gri-gri* lamps bobbed far off, and further still shepherds' watch-fires flickered on the Albanian hills.

In between were the midday hours, when the heat drove us under the shade of the verandah and, after lunch, to our beds. A noon breeze ruffled the surface of the sea and turned it to a bright blue. An occasional caique with a cargo of watermelons might chug up from Lefkimmi in the south, or the small white shape of the Athens boat creep almost imperceptibly along the faint outline of the mainland. How empty the gulf would have seemed to those who knew it when it was the sea-lane of the Venetian Empire, and Corfu was the key to the Adriatic, and the hill above Chlomos got its name of Merovigli – the Daytime Lookout.

History has passed this way, in the form of famous armadas. The triremes and penteconters of the Athenian expedition against Syracuse passed up the gulf after their voyage round the Peloponnese. Corcyra was their last port of call before the crossing to Sicily, and the sailors and hoplites must have drunk in the waterfront taverns of the Hyllaic harbour – now the lagoon by the airport – and told the townsmen of the brave setting forth from Piraeus, the silver trumpets calling the whole fleet to pour a libation to the gods, and the ships racing each other across the Saronic to Aegina, confidently ignorant of how it was all to end in disease and starvation in the Syracusan stone quarries.

Fifth century Athens's explosion of genius had just set the Greek world ablaze. Some sixteen hundred years later, the last flickers of the the old Hellenism were still bright enough to divert the Fourth Crusade from its proper goal to Constantinople. The decision was finally reached on Corfu, for not all the knights had yet been persuaded to betray the cause for which they had taken the Cross. Geoffrey de Villehardouin, the chronicler of the crusade, describes the assembly at which the old blind doge fell on his knees and begged the waverers not to desert him. A few went their own way to Outremer, but the main body followed the Venetian lead and set sail for the city on the Eve of Pentecost 1204. The wind was fair, Villehardouin records, and the day fine, and with much joy in their hearts they sailed away from the town, the fleet covering the waters of the gulf, a splendid sight to see.

The third major war-fleet to pass the same way – one which was heading for neither disaster nor disgrace – was that led against the Turks by Don John of Austria, Philip II of Spain's lively bastard half-brother. Ottoman power in the Mediterranean had reached its zenith. Six years earlier, in 1565, Malta, under the Knights of St John, had only just survived a long and terrible siege. The Turkish admiral Ochiali (a renegade Greek from Calabria) was ravaging the coasts and islands of the Ionian and Adriatic. At last, in September 1571, a Christian fleet assembled at Corfu, composed of squadrons from Spain, Venice and the Papal states. On the 30th there sailed down past Benitses and Mesonghi towards Igoumenitsa more than 200 oared galleys, and 30 to 40 sailing warships – galleasses, frigates and brigantines – manned by 50,000 mariners and galley slaves. On Sunday 7 October Don John's fleet all but annihilated the Turkish fleet off Nafpaktos (which the west Europeans called Lepanto) and freed some 15,000 Christian galley slaves. On the 24th the expedition sailed back up the gulf, to three days of wild celebration in Corfu town.

(It is said that as the battle was on the point of beginning, Don John and his senior officers danced a cool defiant galliard on the quarter-deck of the flagship. It is a known fact that an officer on the *Marquesa,* who insisted on fighting in spite of a fever, and was wounded three times, was one Miguel de Cervantes, who later adopted a literary career.)

The river was like an extra dimension. Streams with more than a trickle of water at the height of summer are rare in Greece. Corfu has three, all where there is flat land on the east coast. The other two are at Potamos, just north of the town, and at Lefkimmi in the south. A variation of our activities, especially when visitors had to be amused, was to board the *Glaros* and row round to the mouth, and then upstream as far as the bamboos below the bridge, beyond which the river was no longer navigable. On the muddy banks close to the village, water-tortoises often sunned themselves and would plop out of sight at our approach, but further up, winding between high, bramble-tangled banks, it could have been a sluggish southern English stream, but for glimpses of olive foliage and the lone pomegranate tree glowing with ruddy fruit. In the evening, fish rose for flies, and provided a livelihood for the kingfishers which shot up and down the river like burnished darts.

The river is more formidable during the winter rains, and can leap into startling spate after one of the thunderstorms of late summer. Ionian storms can be very sudden. They had a habit of waking us in the small hours, and sending the whole household down the beach in nighties and underpants to draw up the boats, to celestial stage effects of thunder and lightning, crashing waves and a tearing wind. One exceptional storm continued for nearly forty-eight hours. By the end of that time the river had burst its banks and turned the olive grove into a lake, at the edge of which the house stood like an island. The main stream carried with it all unattached objects within reach, and swept out to sea an assortment of branches, bamboo stems, melon rinds and household rubbish, which, after a graceful U-turn, it deposited on the shore in front of our house, creating a three-foot high bank between us and the water.

Among the beach shingle one could find, here and there, small flakes of flint. Augustus Sordinas, who knows everything about the pre-history of Corfu, pointed these out and identified them as the waste from tool-making by palaeolithic men, who inhabited the island thirty to forty thousand years ago. I liked to imagine my beetle-browed ancestors sitting on our very shore and delighting in the same view, as they fashioned their hand-axes. Augustus, however, disillusioned me. Europe was then just emerging from the last Ice Age. The level of the oceans was much lower than it is today. Corfu was joined to the mainland, and Mesonghi nowhere near the sea. The flints had almost certainly been washed down by the river over the millennia, from further inland. The nearest palaeolithic settlement was a shallow cave on the hillside above Gardiki between the village of Ay. Mathia and the Korissia lagoon. Excavations have revealed the bones of the animals hunted by the old tool-makers. These included giant deer, horses and oxen, which populated cold climate forests of birch and alder, a landscape entirely different from the present.

Gardiki itself is a dilapidated and heavily overgrown thirteenth-century fort. Its masonry is layered with thin courses of brick, in the Byzantine style. Close by, a spring of clear water used to well up from below a rock, topped by an olive tree. This fed a pool, haunted by dragonflies of many colours and used by the people of Ay. Mathia to water their beasts. Its existence may have determined the siting of the fort and – who knows? – provided water for the hunters of the cave. Now they have shut up the naiad of the spring in a nasty little concrete house and put her in charge of the district mains supply, and the pool and its jewelled insects are no more.

Apart from the kingfishers, we had few birds. A rare hoopoe might pay a surprise visit, strutting for a while among the sparse shore plants, before taking off, like a great inconsequential butterfly, in search of richer pastures. The bay had no wading birds at all, and even gulls came only in ones and twos. Clearly there was none of the good feeding that fills the Korissia lagoon with oystercatcher, plover, sandpiper and stilt, as well as many varieties of duck, heron, gull and tern. The Greek summer is not the best time for observing small land birds, but, even so, the shortage of them, other than sparrows, in and near the village was surprising.

Instead of swallows and house martins we had rats. At the time that we were creating and moving into the house we never saw one, but soon after we first arrived they made their presence known above our heads, scuttling over the bamboos of the ceiling. It became clear that they must have nested in the roof for many generations, when the building was used for storage and olive-pressing, and had no intention of losing their ancestral home. Where they came from and how they found their way into the roof, we never discovered. We stopped up every possible entrance, but still they got in. We laid nylon sheets on the bamboos and put down poison. This seemed to be effective, for the sounds of movement would cease for a week or two. Then, one siesta hour, there would come a plop on the nylon and soon they would be engaged again in what sounded like games of rat-football. No solution to the problem was ever found, but at least our rats were discreet. We never saw one alive and rarely found a corpse.

The only other indoor resident was a spider which lodged in a crack in the plaster of our bedroom wall and must have fasted during our stays, for it made no web and was never seen to emerge. Geckos frequented the verandah, and a pair of crickets were in permanent occupation of the ligaria bush beside the millstone. The male's gentle chirp made an agreeable accompaniment to the evening ouzo. The ligaria, or chaste tree, is common near the sea in Greece. It bears long spikes of purple flowers, with seeds like peppercorns. These give it its nickname of monk's pepper, being used in monasteries in place of real pepper, which inflames the carnal passions. Thus the plant is a badge of chastity. The stems of our bush were thickly encrusted with tiny snails. During the hot season these were unmoved by carnal or any other passion. They simply withdrew into their shells and did not stir until the first rain. Then the colony began to heave and slither to the ground in search of food, gradually returning as the moisture dried up. One summer a pair of whitethroats nested in the base of the ligaria, their domestic activity going unnoticed until they emerged with six newly fledged chicks.

Dogs moved in and out of our life. Like all the villages. Mesonghi had a population of sturdy mongrels, each with its individual appearance and personality, but collectively a set of variations on the basic village-dog theme. They all had owners, but Greek villagers are unsentimental about animals and value dogs for their usefulness in guarding property rather than as pets, nor did most households have much food to spare for feeding them. As a result the animals spent much of their time in foraging and soon discovered that our house was a good source of scraps. Our first summer we made the mistake of allowing ourselves to be adopted by Moritsa, a beguiling bitch with an elegant figure, suggesting that she might have had an Irish setter as a grandmother. She started to live in and around the house and almost at once came on heat. Within a few days we were besieged day and night by a ring of dogs, either fighting each other or howling with frustration. This lasted until Moritsa bestowed her favours on the top dog and even he was savagely attacked, in the act of copulation, by a defeated rival.

We never saw Moritsa's puppies, but some time later another bitch had a litter of three in the space at the base of a hollow olive tree. She showed signs of being unable to feed them and of losing interest, so our daughter Amanda rescued the three pups and set up a crèche in the house. The two dog puppies scrapped all the time and were christened Cassius Clay and Sonny Liston, this being the year when the former (later Mohammed Ali) took the world heavyweight title from the latter. Cassius left the village, but Sonny stayed on to become a tough local veteran. He was mildly eccentric. objected to being photographed, and used to appear out of the olives, pad down the beach, and stand for a few minutes cooling his feet in the sea. To the end he kept an eye on us. At the end of our holiday he always knew we were driving away for good and ran beside the car as far as the bridge.

However well we got to know the people – and we became quite friendly with Maria and her family, and with the Rossis – there was always a distance between us. We and they were on opposite sides of the divide separating the worlds of the villages and the towns. This was not so much a division between the classes as between two forms of society, the one peasant, soil-based and governed by all manner of unchanging customs and superstitions, the other restless, commercial and enterprising. One of its manifestations was a difference in the mode of address. In 'polite society', Greeks, like the

French, use the plural forms 'you' and 'your' when speaking to another person, keeping the singular 'thou', 'thee' and 'thy' for conversation with relatives and close friends. Villagers use the forms correctly, singular for one person, plural for more than one, when speaking among themselves. A villager does not expect to be spoken to as 'you' even by a stranger; he finds this confusing rather than flattering. On the other hand, he will, as a matter of politeness, use the plural form to a 'non-villager'. Thus in converse with our neighbours one side said 'you' and the other 'thou', without any awkwardness.

Our use of the house as a holiday home – particularly as members of the local big landowners – probably roused some resentment, though we lived plainly enough and did our best to be tactful. On the whole, it seems more likely that our comings and goings were treated as irrelevant. We were there so little that it would have been impertinent for us to try to become involved in village affairs, and I remember only one occasion when I played a minor role, by request.

A neighbour's wife came to ask a favour. Her son was about to marry a girl from Strongyli, three or four miles away. The wedding ceremony was to be at the bride's village church, the festivities afterwards at the groom's parents' house. A lorry had been hired to bring the guests from Strongyli to Mesonghi. Would it be an imposition, she wondered, if she asked me, since we had a car, to be chauffeur to the happy couple? It would not. I inquired about the hour for collection. There was the usual Corfiot vagueness as to the times of church services, but it was thought that they should be coming out of church about noon.

It was mid-August. The fifteenth – the Feast of the Dormition – sees the beginning of a great season for weddings. The morning was very hot. I drove to Strongyli at the appointed time. Far from coming out of church, the maiden was still in her family house, being attired by her sisters and friends. I was offered and accepted a small, very sweet liqueur, flavoured with banana. The bridal attendants finished their task and sang a hymeneal chorus. They then descended to the courtyard, where a band of violin, concertina and drum was waiting. Led by the musicians, we made a tuneful procession to the church. The service was no different from my own marriage, except that it was even hotter, and the priest had to break off continually to pronounce anathemas on unruly children. At the end, the bride and groom sat on chairs at the church door, and wedding gifts, mostly of money, were placed in her lap.

We were fiddled and drummed back to the main road. The guests piled into a lorry and were driven off. I duly followed in state with the pair and the priest. At the house, a couple of hundred yards from our own, I was given another drink and asked if I would stay to eat. I was not – and to this day am not – sure if the correct answer to the question was yes or no, but decided that it was better to cause embarrassment than off-ence. We went into the large plain room which occupied the ground floor of the house and sat down on benches at two long bare tables. The two families eyed each other with the dark suspicion to be found on such occasions in every land. The meal began in a strained silence. It was hotter than ever.

As a starter we drank mutton broth, piping hot and greasy, served with hunks of dark country bread and tumblers of rough wine. This was followed by gobbets of boiled mutton, and next by gobbets of roast mutton and potatoes. I was provided with a knife and fork. The others ate with their fingers. To get this down our throats, it was necessary to drink copious quantities of wine. Very soon we were all laughing, talking and dripping with sweat. When we had put away huge segments of water-melon as a dessert, covering our faces with juice from ear to ear, the fiddler began to doodle softly on his strings, and revelry was clearly immi-nent. 'Why is the lady not here?' they demanded; 'Will you not go and call her?' 'I will bring her,' I said. 'Much later,' I said to myself. It must have been about half past four. I stumbled home along the shore, fell on my bed, and went into a stupor for two hours.

Eleven

Changes were overdue and, to begin with, all for the better. Public water was laid on to Mesonghi. At first it had to be drawn from standpipes, but at least the women no longer had to make their daily trips to the spring. Later, it was piped to those houses that wanted it, and our well went out of use. After the water came the electricity. Lamps and candles were for emergencies only. Mitso Rossi installed a village telephone in his shop. It was of the type, sometimes shown in very old films, which involves the rapid turning of a handle to call the exchange, but one could, usually after an hour's delay in getting a line, on most days get a call through to town, or sometimes even to Athens. We did not encourage friends to ring us up. By the time that Mitso's daughter, Marina, had come along the beach to fetch us to the phone, the caller had almost inevitably been cut off.

The road was extended (without asphalt) behind our house to the other half of the village, and subsequently as far as Kodhraka point. Gradually, small holiday houses with gardens appeared along the bay. Mitso set up an open-air restaurant opposite the old café, and for several seasons we ate absurdly cheap meals there, well cooked by Marina and her mother, and served by a cheerful young waiter called Stefano. Another restaurant, the Ramos, opened at the other end. Mitso then built an eight-roomed *pension* at the sea's edge, alongside his restaurant, and his neighbour, Andreana, also began to let rooms. The village started to look prosperous.

My father-in-law was soon impressed by what we had made of the *litrouvio* and revised his gloomy ideas about Mesonghi. He restored the main house and planted a vegetable garden, and from then on moved in beside us every summer. We planted oleanders and poplars round the two houses, which grew so vigorously that we achieved considerable privacy from the public gaze.

All this reflected, in miniature, what was going on all over the island. The town acquired a new high-class hotel, the Corfu Palace on Garitsa Bay, designed by Elisabeth's father, Pericles Sakellarios. The same company opened the Miramare, a hotel with bungalows, near us on the bay beyond Moraitika. Several others opened north of the town. The Club Méditerranée established itself at Dasia, while a wealthy German, Baron von Richthofen, took a lease of the Achillion Palace, and rescued it from desolation and decay by turning it into a gambling casino. This may have distressed the spirit of the Empress Elisabeth, but it brought employment to many more inhabitants of Gastouri, which as the adjacent village provided a large part of the staff, from croupiers to gardeners.

By this time, of course, the channel between Corfu and Albania had for some years been open to shipping. The first big car ferries, the *Appia* and *Egnatia,* began to ply between Brindisi, Corfu and Patras. Summer visitors from Europe, especially Italians, for the first time came to Corfu in large numbers. The north of the island ceased to be a restricted area. Land was still comparatively cheap – its price had not long ceased to be fixed by the number of olive trees on the property, and owners took a little time to appreciate its enormous development value. The climate and beauty of Corfu, combined with the, then, low cost of living, attracted many foreigners, mostly British, to buy land and to live for all or part of the year in Corfu. (It was still officially a frontier area, in which foreigners were not allowed to buy land. Various devices for circumventing this law were resorted to, all unsatisfactory and sources of legal complications.)

Corfu was for some years a superior and fashionable resort. It drew additional cachet from the fact that the Greek royal family re-opened, and spent holidays in, the small summer palace of Mon Repos. It became the habit of prime ministers to stay at the Miramare Hotel. The Mesonghites got some benefit from this in the form of repairs to the coast road from town. Tar spreaders and road rollers were a sure sign that an *episimos,* or VIP, would soon be passing that way.

These developments were scarcely affected by the political events of the time, which took a dramatic turn. By the early 1960s it was possible to sense both a growing desire for social reform, and a feeling that the monarchy (non-Greek in origin, and imposed on the young Hellenic state by the European powers) had become anachronistic and irrelevant. The right-wing governments of Papagos and Karamanlis lost support, and some years of political instability followed. The voices of the Communists and their sympathisers, muted since the civil war, grew louder and more confident. Karamanlis refused to play the game of forming coalition governments, and retired to a de Gaulle-like isolation in France. The parliamentarians continued to put party and personal ambition before country.

The Army lost patience. On the night of 21 April 1967 a group of officers and the units under their command took over the streets of Athens and the broadcasting system with tanks and guns. They issued a decree, bearing to be in the king's name, which suspended the constitution and imposed martial law. So began the seven-year dictatorship of the junta of 'the colonels' – the *'Hounda'.* The young King Constantine (who had succeeded his father Paul in 1964) did not in fact sign the decree, though he was much blamed for not declaring his immediate disapproval of his own officers' unconstitutional behaviour. Too late, he involved himself, that December, in a counter-coup by officers opposed to the colonels. It failed, and Constantine was obliged to flee the country. It was the effectual end of monarchy in Greece.

There was something Cromwellian about the colonels. Men of simple and narrow faith, they proclaimed themselves as authors of a 'Helleno-Christian civilisation' – a concept which others found obscure. In this they were probably genuine, but being rather less than clever (Brigadier Patakos's intellectual capacity was an abundant source of merriment in the capital), totally intolerant of all points of view but their own, inimical to socialists and deeply contemptuous of politicians, they adopted the time-honoured methods of dictators everywhere. Parliament was suspended; trade unions were banned; the press was censored; broadcasting was controlled by the state; even private freedom of speech was cutailed by a wide network of secret police and informers. Nasty tales of police brutality went around – though, as Marily used to point out to non-Greek friends, this was nothing new, either in Greece or elsewhere.

Democrats all over the world deplored the situation, but so long as the government of the United States needed Greece as a useful member of NATO, the colonels were safe, only bringing about their own downfall by a foolish involvement in the Cypriot debacle which ended with a Turkish invasion. Some sensitive philhellenes refused to visit Greece, while the begetter of democracy was being subjected to such indignities. This however was not really a practical option for those to whom Greece was their other country. We continued to go regularly to Corfu, and found that, at least for anyone visiting on a foreign passport, the regime made no difference to life or its enjoyment.

They were, in fact, the best years. The children being older, we could range further afield both on and outside the island. With George and Elena Manessi and their family, we made expeditions by caique to most of the nearby islands – Mathraki and Erikousa, Paxi and Antipaxi, and as far as Lefkada. George's sailing experience, apparently infinite circle of friends, and energetic good humour made marvellous memories of these voyages. The Lefkada venture was part of an attempt to reach Ithaca, foiled by the breakdown of one of the boat's pumps. In the event we spent two nights at

Lefkada, one moored off a point where the scholar Dorpfeld lies buried, having maintained to his dying day that Odysseus' Ithaca was not the modern island of that name, but the near-island of Lefkada. We lay the second night in the port, where a cultural festival was advertised as taking place, with visiting orchestras and ballets from various European countries. Unfortunately, financial and other reasons had prevented most of them from reaching the Ionian, and we had to make do with a regional clarinet competition. From the applause, the prize was clearly destined for the player able to sustain the longest single note on one breath.

All over Greece roads were being re-engineered and surfaced, air services extended, car ferries introduced, harbours deepened and improved. There also came into being a first generation of regional hotels, classified and controlled by the authorities, with beds, food and plumbing considered suitable for foreign tourists. All this made travelling much easier, though less eventful. Marily and I, sometimes on our own and at others with family or friends, visited the islands of Crete, Aegina, Spetses, Ydra, Lesbos and Siphnos, and, on the mainland, explored the main sites of the Peloponnese – Olympia, Sparta, Mistra, Mycenae and Epidaurus – and spent a few days in the distinctive world of the Mount Pelion peninsula, where the villages are set among apple orchards and chestnut forests, and are all of stone, even to the heavy slabbed roofs.

It was a voyage of discovery for us both, for the occupation and its aftermath had prevented Marily from enjoyng the richness and variety of her own land. The failure to reach Ithaca, and the postponement of that arrival until many years later, came to be seem symbolic. Cavafy had said that the journey there ought to be long, full of vicissitudes and insights. In a way, Corfu was becoming our Ithaca. Unexpectedly, the more I absorbed of Greece, the stronger grew the pull of our island. My system must have become accustomed to whatever it was that had made me feel unwell, and little by little I lost the craving for Apollo's blue and golden Aegean. Instead, I began to yearn in Athens for the tender harmony of the Corfiot landscape and the cypresses marching like spearmen up the olive-silver hills. I could understand at last why Marily's father was so reluctant ever to leave the place, and, like George Manessi, I felt the lift of the heart as the plane began its descent down the gulf, and the familiar dark outline took shape above the mirror of the sea.

Of course, we did not keep Mesonghi entirely to ourselves. Marily's mother often stayed there with us, and an increasing number of friends from Scotland – and their children and their friends – came to relax and amuse themselves in the house on the beach, either as our guests or on holiday on their own. To give pleasure to others there added to our pleasure in this paradise we had created.

Tourism was getting more sophisticated, but there was still much that remained odd and innocent. At Dasia, the lobster restaurant tethered the creatures to the uprights of the jetty. You walked out with the owner to inspect his flock where it crawled on the sandy bottom, chose one to be hauled up kicking on its string, and then had a swim while it was boiled alive for your lunch. The traditional place for sampling lobsters – more correctly, langoustes, which had not yet been priced out of the everyday market – was Paleocastritsa. One restaurateur lured the English with a sign advertising FRESH LAMBSTERS. On the Ay. Deka road a large, uncouth man with an underhung jaw, named Matthaios, ran a 'butcher's taverna', serving nothing but meat. This had to be ordered, not by the helping but by weight, and was put on the table in large chunks on greaseproof paper. It was washed down with jugfuls of Matthaios's own robust red wine. Unfortunately the wine was its maker's staple diet and made his face ever more fiery until, to popular regret, it finished him off.

The roadside café at Moraitika, run by a local character with the Karaghiozi nickname of 'Gnio-gnio', blossomed into Charlie's Bar. Charlie could both lift a table with his teeth and dance with a tumbler of water balanced on his head, and drew much custom. He installed the first of the juke-boxes which became the scourge of our area, and used this in instructing his foreign clientele in simple Greek dances. These convivial classes took place on the road outside the bar, and were a nightly feature of the neighbourhood until the police decided that they were too much of a peril to both drivers and dancers.

Behind the Mesonghi olive groves, the land rises gently towards a graceful old house with a big walled courtyard, and a disused private chapel. A carved inscription over the tall stone gateway declares that it was built in the eighteenth century by a member of the Trivoli family. (The house has long since passed into other hands, and is now extended and converted into holiday apartments.) There is a neglected mixed orchard of quince, apricot and almond, and beside this the village decided, at last, to build its own church. The work went on in fits, according to the state of the funds, during most of our years at Mesonghi. At one point it seemed to have been abandoned altogether, but the growing trickle of new money produced a spurt of activity and the completion of the roof. A couple of seasons later the altar, the *iconostasis* and all the sacred pictures and other church furnishings were in place, and the parish church of Mesonghi was ready for dedication.

It was a very little church, but it needed a full-scale priest. To this end, the devout Spiro, in a sound biblical tradition, was taken from his calling as a fisher for *kefalous*, and ordained as *papas* of his native village. We attended the pack-ed inaugural service, at which Papa Spiro first officiated. At the end, he preached a fervent denunciation of tourism, likening it unto the Red Beast of the Apocalypse which rose out of the sea and uttered blasphemies. This fanaticism sur-prised us until we realised that Spiro the Fish was taking advantage of his new status to give vent to his feelings about the Bulgaris, Manessis, Damaskini and other landowning families who were able to enrich themselves by building and managing large hotels. He can have had little idea of how accurate his imagery was to prove in the ensuing years.

The turning-point, of course, was the enlargement of the airport. The new terminal building and lengthened runway made it capable of handling large planes, flying direct from West European cities. The package tour operators moved into action according to well laid plans. I was shown, at the time, an article in a travel industry trade magazine, predicting that within ten years nobody from Britain would be able to take a holiday in Corfu except as part of a chartered flight package. The Corfiots cooperated wholeheartedly in the conversion of their island to a Greek Mallorca or Costa Brava. More hotels were built each year, more and more houses modernised for letting, more tavernas, cafés, bars and shops opened.

In town, the street of the Saint, where trade had been restricted to the sale of religious medallions and votive candles, became lined with shops crammed with mass-produced imitation antiques, factory-made folk objects and bottles of koum-kwat liqueur, and draped with T-shirts legended in doubtful taste.

At Mesonghi a gigantic box of a hotel sprang up on the other side of the river, with a terrace directly above the mud bank where the water-tortoises had been accustomed to sun themselves. Every night the music provided by the management to deafen the guests flooded into our bedroom till one or two in the morning. The Rossi hotel grew in size and splendour. The villagers extended their houses outwards and upwards, and began to offer rooms to let. Among others, Spiro the Pump and his brother opened a pleasant little restaurant named The Stars, where old Maria now spent most of the day, washing dishes and peeling potatoes for chips with everything. One local boy acquired a speedboat and set himself up as a water-ski instructor. We sold the *Glaros* for a modest sum to Spiro, who used it for excursions.

It was tolerable at first, and indeed agreeable to see the village come to life, however seasonal and artificial. The summer visitors mostly kept to the ends of the beach, by the two halves of the village. In the early morning, and again in the evening, our shore was practically as quiet and beautiful as it always had been. The most unpleasant aspect was a gradual deterioration in standards of behaviour. The Mesonghites were no more scrupulous in business than any other Corfiots, but they were no thieves. Personal belongings could be left about completely safely, and the only times when a door or window in the village was locked was at the approach of gypsies. The gypsies had been moving around the island for at least seven centuries, resolute in their refusal to adopt settled ways. Today they drive huge lorries and hawk all sorts of goods, from second-hand furniture to water melons. Twenty years ago they still went on foot, with strings of lean horses, and plied some sort of trade as tin and copper smiths. The women, thin and dark of face, in long, garishly coloured skirts, usually accompanied by two or three lovely, filthy children, are inveterate beggars. They have whining voices and contemptuous eyes, and smoke cigarettes openly in the street. The villages' dislike and fear of them was almost superstitious in its intensity. Hens and turkeys were closely guarded till they had passed on. With the arrival of the tourists, it was necessary to be careful all the time. Bikinis mysteriously vanished from washing lines. A beach umbrella left unattended was likely to be treated as public property. Once, when we returned after an absence of two weeks, we found the house broken into, and two strange girls in residence.

Some of the foreigners – mostly, but not all, British – introduced new permissive standards of sexual behaviour to Corfu. The villagers were not puritanical. The old practice of displaying the wedding night bedsheets at the window in the morning, to testify to the bride's virginity, had become a dead-letter and a joke. As in many rural communities, a couple liked to be certain that the union was going to be fertile before announcing a formal engagement. But, outside that prudent convention, a girl's honour was precious, and a promiscuous daughter brought shame on herself and her family. The fair, easygoing girls from the north were at the same time desired and despised.

One evening, returning from one of our sea-going trips, and dressed accordingly, Marily and Elena were walking from the port to the Manessi house in town. They became aware of being followed by two young soldiers of the Greek Army, whistling at them and making suggestive remarks. Marily eventually rounded on them and told them that they ought to be ashamed of themselves. The boys sprang to attention and looked abashed. 'Forgive us, lady,' one of them said, 'we are very sorry. We thought you were English.'

The next summer, I was wakened in the night by sounds of movement outside our bedroom window. On opening the shutters to find out if we were being burgled, I discovered, by the light of a brilliantly romantic moon, an English couple in the act of making love on the verandah. This finally decided us that it was time to find somewhere else to take the place of Mesonghi.

Twelve

Gastouri had receded – maybe we had pushed it – to the periphery of our Corfu experience. The old house was destined to be the inheritance of Marily's brother Stevie. (His twin, Nicky, had died in a road accident, leaving Anne, his French wife, with one small daughter.) In the summers, when we were all staying in the two Mesonghi houses, it was shut, only opened up on special occasions, such as a family christening or the traditional party for Marily's birthday. Otherwise we scarcely ever went there except to show it to visitors from Britain and to raid the lemon trees in the secret, dappled garden.

We had stayed in the house once since that first time after our wedding. At Eastertide of 1966, Marily's half-sister Elisabeth – following the family trend in international alliances – married an Austrian fellow-architect. We took the children to Corfu for this celebration, and borrowed the Gastouri house for our stay. Like most Mediterranean country houses at that time, it was shiveringly unsuitable for cold weather habitation and felt like a vault after an unfired winter. We kept an enormous log fire burning for three days in the fireplace beneath the cracked looking-glass, and even then needed five layers of blankets in the bedrooms.

It was my first spring in Corfu, and it seemed like a new land, reviving memories of the encampment beside the Gulf of Lamia a score of years before. Corfu was even greener, the anemones and irises and asphodel more prolific. Everywhere the bare branches of the Judas trees were breaking into purple-pink blossom, and a white star shone at each tip of the quinces. The garden was transformed, but not by the hand of man. Flowers of the field, whose existence I had never suspected, took over and reigned undisturbed. At the height of the florescence I took a census and picked no fewer than forty-five wild species in bloom.

I got to know the main characters who peopled the stage of our near neighbourhood. In a house loking on to the back courtyard lived Leonidas and Leni,* the more-or-less honorary guardians of the property. Leonidas was a skilful gardener and olive cultivator, but fonder of ouzo than of hard work. Leni was industrious, unassuming and one of the best-hearted women one could hope to meet. She was illiterate and had a local reputation as a simpleton. Unkind mimics could cause much village ribaldry with well-embroidered impersonations of Leni fending off Leonidas's advances on their wedding night – they had in fact no children – and later, when Greek women got the vote, we all, I regret, made merry at the news that she had mistaken her husband's directions and put into the ballot box, instead of her voting paper, their electricity bill. She took all ribbing in good part, and enlivened her fairly elementary conversation with a stock of well-worn jokes, such as referring to Poppy her donkey as 'the Mercedes', and refusing offers of refreshment by declaring herself a non-smoker.

The Kamareli family lived where the road ended just below the house. Old Tsanda, the grandmother, passed most of her days crocheting outside her door, with her vast form overflowing a stone bench. All comings and goings by the road came under her scrutiny. She was very fond of Marily, whom she invariably greeted with ecstatic cries of 'My pride, my doll', and enveloped in her bosom's wide embrace. Acquiring popularity by association, I also got to know that region well. Her son, Spiro, was a small quiet cultivator, married to Nina, a strong dark girl with a voice like a peahen, who looked as if she could eat him for breakfast but, surpri-

* Short for Eleni, i.e. Helen. Very many Greek girls bear the name, not after the gorgeous reason for the Trojan war, but in honour of Saint Helen, mother of Constantine the Great, sanctified for her discovery of the True Cross.

singly, always spoke of her husband as 'the master'. Our other nearest neighbour was Vasili, a dignified and courtly villager of the old school, who was a carpenter by trade, but best known, for many years, as the director of the 'Mousiki', the Gastouri town band. He demanded a high standard of both performance and behaviour, and made it an honour to belong to, and a disgrace to be dismissed from, the band. The daily round brought us into touch with fat Kotso, who kept the dark, jumbled general store; Spiro of the Meeting Place café, where much of the male population passed their days; and serious Hector, the village baker, whose *fourno* produced – and still produces – the best bread on the island.

We had a good friend in our parish priest, our own Papa Spiro (more familiarly Papa Pipi), whose formal name was Father Perdikas, which means 'Partridge'. He looked like a plump brown bird, and was a real man of the community, growing up in Gastouri and known to Marily as a boy in the pre-war summers which she spent there. His jurisdiction covered the churches of both Gastouri and Pahatika, as well as various chapels in the surrounding countryside, which had to be ministered to once a year, as each celebrated its feast. His headquarters was our local church.

The houses and courtyards and gardens of Gastouri spill, higgledy-piggledy, threaded by narrow alleys and stairways, down the hillside both above and below the main road. The church stands at the very bottom, in the old secret heart of the village, on a small plateau above the final plunge into the ravine. It is a light-hearted building, well tended and appointed. It is dedicated to Mary, the Mother of God, in her aspect of the Panayia Odhiyitria – the All-Holy Guide, or, as Westerners might say, Our Lady of Guidance. She is an important lady in the village, and her icon – the traditional Odhiyitria Madonna, pointing to her Child and gazing sad-eyed at the world – is, for the Orthodox of Gastouri, her local habitation. It is also something of a mobile home, for our Odhiyitria is a travelling lady. She is given full honours on her feast day in August. The band comes into church and plays a special piece of solemn music to her, and she is then carried in procession round the whole village. Her banner leads, followed by a double file of little girls, in their best dresses, scattering rose petals from baskets. The band and church choir precede her, playing and chanting alternately, the priest walks behind her, and the people bring up the rear. On Easter Monday she is similarly escorted to the chapel of Kopanous, about half a mile away, and presides over the liturgy there, and a few days later she pays her annual visit to the Pahatika church of St Nicholas, returning home on the Vigil of the Ascension.

The wedding was arranged for Easter Monday. Before that, we had the whole of the Great Week, with its Corfiot variations. On Palm Sunday we all went into town for the Saint's first *litania* of the year, which is also the longest of his peregrinations round the town. The procession – brass bands, schools, Guides, Scouts and all – circles the upper and lower esplanades (in April, rose-pink with the flower of the Judas trees, from one of which the Iscariot is said to have hanged himself*) and passes down the sea walls of the Mourayia to the Old Port, before making its way back to the great church by the back streets. The slow march, and the long halts for prayers, place a heavy strain on the participants, especially the children.

On Great Friday, the Epitaphion – the symbolic funeral bier of the dead Christ – was decorated with flowers of all colours and set in the centre of the Odhiyitria's church, as in all Orthodox churches, to receive its plain wooden crucifix. Throughout the day, which was dull and overcast, every village campanile tolled a passing bell for the death of God, oppressing the senses with their insistent melancholy. In the evening, after dark, our church was packed with worshippers, all holding lighted candles, for the long hymn which

* A medieval legend, possibly deriving from the fact that an ancient name for Corfu was Scheria, held that Judas Iscariot was a Corfiot. This is without foundation.

148

heralds the procession of the Epitaphion. The women's gallery at the back was a line of handsome, weather-beaten faces and the elaborate ribbon-plaited coiffures of the older women. At last, four men carried the Epitaphion with its crucifix out of church, the band struck up a Dead March, and the river of candle flooded up through the winding lanes to the road and the war memorial at the top of the village.

The next morning we were again in town for the celebration – unique to Corfu – of the Proti Anastasi, the First Resurrection. Proceedings begin at nine o'clock with another procession of the saint. The oldest in origin, it dates from the sixteenth century and commemorates the deliverance of the island from famine. It is combined with a second Epitaphion progress. The town bands take turns in playing the 'Amletto' dead march, from a late French opera about the Prince of Denmark. The *litania* is over by ten. The populace then go home and wait for the Saint's clock to strike eleven. The bells are rung, and everybody hurls an old piece of crockery from the window on to the street and the head of any ignorant stranger who happens to be abroad, crying 'So may our enemies perish!' All then embrace, with the greeting 'Christ is risen' and the response 'He is risen indeed'. Before the war it was also the custom, demonstrating the link between Easter and the Hebrew Passover, to slaughter lambs in the streets and to daub the door lintels with their blood. Private Wheeler described the pot-breaking, with horrid cursing on the Jews, in the 1820s, and went on to add that the Jews of Corfu 'are obliged to keep out of the way until Easter is over, or they would be murdered. The part of the town the Jews occupy is barricaded and they go in and out at two gates. These gates are shut at 9 o'clock through the year, but from Good Friday until Easter holidays are over the Greeks get so devilish religious it is necessary to have a guard of soldiers at each of the gates.'

These excesses are confined to the town. The villages keep the Anastasi, like all other good Christians, till midnight on

Great Saturday, when the new fire is brought out from church, and the Gospel of the Resurrection read in the open, and there is much setting off of firecrackers and other jubilation, followed by a snack of lamb's entrail soup and red hard-boiled eggs. (All this happens too in the town. The bishop reads the Gospel from the bandstand on the upper esplanade, it is broadcast, with the audibility of a British Rail station announcement, to a crowd of several thousand, and the whole thing has become a secular tourist spectacle.)

By Easter Sunday morning Marily and I were hungry. The children had eaten normally during the week, but we had tried to keep to the rules for fasting, which involve abstaining from all meat, fish and dairy produce, and on Wednesday and Friday from any form of fat. On Good Friday it is traditional not to set a table for meals, and to restrict the midday fare to lentil soup, soured with vinegar, olives and boiled potatoes. The regime is not as hard as it sounds. Shellfish, octopus and roe (including caviar) do not count as fish. Anyone with a taste for oysters and lobster can make the best of Greek Holy Week. But the lack of fat produces a powerful sense of emptiness and spirituality. One of our neighbours at Gastouri – another Spiro – came early to the house in pouring rain, made a charcoal fire under cover of a shed roof, impaled a sad naked lamb on an iron spit, and patiently turned it to a golden-brown, crisp-skinned, greasy end to the fast. We filled our stomachs, cracked more red eggs, gazed out at the deluge, and prayed for better weather on the morrow.

Elisabeth and Hermann were married in the monastery church at Paleocastritsa. Some years earlier, her father had built, for himself and her, a house clinging to the hill above a small bay, some way north of the monastery headland. The place could be reached only on foot, either along a stretch of sea-shore and up a woodland path, or, after a boat trip round to the bay, almost perpendicularly up fom the sea. Building materials came to the site on the heads, or in the strong arms, of a gang of women, and sophisticated techniques were ruled out. Yet Sakellarios's personality and imagination created, in this impossible position, a work of daring simplicity and strength.

The house looks out on a scene of powerful beauty, which at night and in time of storm can turn to menace. High cliffs rise sheer on either side of the saddle where the house stands, and stretch far to the north, their faces scarred where old landslides have sent rocks crashing down to lie in gigantic confusion at the sea's edge. The restless Ionian nags incessantly at the coves and points. Almost always there is the noise of the swell running in from Italy and breaking over the rocks. Yet beside the house a small vineyard has been planted, and scrub and cliff flowers have found footholds all the way down to the bay, which has its special population of birds of the rocks.

From this eyrie, Elisabeth's father had had the fancy to bring her, bridally attired, by boat to the main bay, there to glide in past the grotto and step ashore, with luck dry-shod, at the foot of the road to the pinnacled monastery. However, Sunday's rain gave way to a *maistro* wind, the strong nor'wester of the Ionian, and a sea voyage in a small boat was impossible. The bride had to walk down under the olive trees and pick her way along a wave-beaten shore to reach her car. The monastery court was full of wind and sunlight and the pattern of sharp shadows on fresh whitewash. Far below, the dark blue sea was edged with foam and flung spray high towards us. Six sucking pigs twirled on the spits. Costumed girls danced to a fiddler's tunes. It was late afternoon before we dispersed, the abbot vanishing into his quarters with the last little pig under his arm.

The district of Gastouri includes one small mountain, between the village and the shores of the gulf. Its lower slopes, rising beside the Achillion road, are wooded and terraced for cultivation. A couple of hundred feet below the summit it becomes suddenly rocky and precipitous, with typical garigue vegetation. On the level patch of the summit a few cypress trees surround a tiny church, a free-standing belfry and a night beacon as a warning for aircraft.

The church has many hilltop counterparts all over Greece. Most are dedicated to the Prophet Elijah, whose chariot of fire is popularly supposed to have taken off from a mountain. Our patroness, however, is a local martyr of the early church, Ayia Kyriaki. (*'Kyriaki'* is the Greek word for Sunday, but means literally 'belonging to the Lord'; Saint Dominica is perhaps a better translation.) It is a humble place of worship, with crude icons and rickety furnishings, but is a shrine which has attracted much devotion. The Empress Elisabeth believed that she found solace there for her troubled spirit. When she stayed in her Corfu retreat, she regularly climbed to the church to pray, and had a long flight of stone steps built through the olive groves to ease the walk – though she seems to have been undaunted by the last rocky scramble.

The Bulgari family have for many years taken responsibility for the upkeep of the church, and are the keepers of its keys. Marily had been fond of it from her childhood, and felt under an obligation to its saint. Sometimes, when we were at Mesonghi, we used to go, as an act of affectionate piety, to see the sun rise from the top of the hill and light a candle in the church. This involved getting up while it was still pitch dark, and driving, bemused with sleep, along the coast to Benitses and up the steep zig-zags to the Achillion. We would leave our car at the war memorial and then follow in the empress's footsteps as the day slowly flooded into the sky. For all the stiff pull up and the dawn chill, it was always worthwhile. The spiders' whorled webs on the strawberry trees and sage bushes were crystalled with dew, and the hollows in the valley had become ponds and lochans of white mist. Random breaths of wind wrinkled the smooth face of the sea, which grew brighter and brighter till the sun burst from the mountain tops and laid a golden pathway for the homing *gri-gri* boats. Then we would go in and pay our compliments to Kyriaki and leave her a candle flame for company as we returned to the world.

Once a year, in July, she has real company. The evening before, some women from Gastouri (it used to be our Leni's job until her legs got too stiff to take her up the hill) clean the little church and scatter bay leaves on the floor. Quite a number of the young people keep up the tradition of spending the night on the hilltop until the sun has risen. By that time Papa Spiro and his cantors have toiled up, bringing the elements of the mysteries, and the round white loaves which will be blessed and distributed after the service. Soon the bell, vigorously rung by an enthusiastic small boy, sends out its first clamorous summons. The congregation, equipped with candles, drifts up the hill in twos and threes, resting for breath and exchanging the greeting for all festive occasions – *'Chronia polla'*, 'Many years'. They meet, running down with their transistors and baseball caps, young men who have been all night on the hilltop and now are late for work.

Papa Spiro hears a few late confessions, then launches with the psaltes into the initial prayers and psalms. Most of the people, other than the ultra-pious, hang around outside gossiping. The preliminaries of the liturgy are really priest's business, and are protracted. The sun is well up now and the day is promising heat. More and more Gastouriots, and visitors from other villages, keep on appearing over the brow of the hill. Gradually the church fills. By the time we reach the gospel of the Wise and Foolish Virgins, the congregation is overflowing through the single door. The psaltes are in full nasal voice now, the acid modes of the Byzantine chant sweetened by the melodic modifications of the Ionian, but still the very words and music that filled the Great Church at Constantinople five hundred years ago. Their candles, like flaming stalagmites, turn the shabby little church, humble and holy as a stable, into a bright cave of chant and frankincense.

We take our pieces of bread from Papa Spiro's brown

153

hand, emerge into the hot sunlight. The hill smells of sage and origanon. We start down, a little leg-weary with all that standing, but glad that we made the effort. *'Kai tou chronou'* we all wish each other – 'and to the year. Till next year.'

Epilogue

At some point in each of our stays in Corfu we always made a special trip to Vasiliko. This is a property, with olive trees of course, on high ground above the long, flat strip of country known as the Val di Ropa. From its western rim you look down at the south end of the valley, where they have now made a golf course, and beyond that to the gap on the hills which leads to Ermones bay and the pools where Nausicaa and her companions washed the royal linen. At the other edge there is a house with a terrace from which, across the island, it is just possible to make out the town.

Vasiliko was a Giallina property, belonging to Marily's grandmother and her two sisters, and the reason why we went to it so often was that there was an understanding – old Corfiots are reluctant to lose control of their possessions, and superstitious about making their wills – that one day it was to be Marily's. The house was shabby and its rooms small, almost poky, and the sanitation was no less primitive than at Gastouri in the old days. The olives were poor and ill-tended, the almond trees, which had once been the glory of the place, both for blossom and for crop, had dried up and ceased to yield, the road was long, steep and in terrible condition, and the house had, except for one uncertain well, neither water nor electricity. But it, and its big outbuildings, were sound enough, and could have been combined, with time and money, into a dwelling of style and beauty. Even in decay and neglect the house and its setting were full of grace and easy elegance. Marily had known and loved and set her heart on Vasiliko from her childhood. Soon her dream became mine also.

For reasons not worth going into, the dream came to

nothing. As the years went by, it became increasingly plain that the restoration of Vasiliko was beyond us, and eventually we had to tell the family that we must look elsewhere. The house is still empty and desolate, and looks at us with reproach.

It has, we believe, turned out for the best. In the end we came back to Gastouri. Perhaps the Odhiyitria and Ayia Kyriaki thought that we would be happier and safer among friends than on a lonely hilltop – why light all those candles, if one is not to be properly looked after?

There was no house for us to take over, but there was a piece of land, mostly a steep slope, covered with scrub and broom and Judas trees, setting it on fire with colour in springtime, but level at the top, with a half-derelict *litrouvio* and old olive trees and a view all round from Ay. Deka to Peleka and, beyond the town and Ypsos bay, the twin peaks of Pantokratora and, on a clear day, the jagged profile of Albania.

So we have created a house of our own, with a terrace built round an olive tree under the shade of which to drink ouzo and eat *fistikia* (pistachio nuts), with half the north of the island laid out before us. Elisabeth made the inspired drawings for the long, low house we asked for, filled with spacious tranquillity. At the laying of the first foundation stone, as required by a tradition of unimaginable antiquity, a white cockerel was ceremonially slaughtered, and its head thrown into the trench. The family and the village neighbours then feasted. The foundations were designed to resist earthquake shocks, the roof was fitted with solar heating panels, and, Papa Spiro having been forced by arthritis to retire, his successor Father Anastasios blessed every part comprehensively, Stefano the building contractor assisting as thurifer and psaltis. Nothing has been left to chance.

The village looks much the same as it did twenty, even forty, years ago. The main road winds as steeply and narrowly as ever between the old houses, and is subject to immovable jamming by the coaches which carry tours to see the Teutonic extravagances of the Achillion. The older men continue to pass the day at the Meeting Place café. The women still sit sewing and chatting on the doorsteps in the evening. But progress, if it has not quite crumbled the cake of custom, is nibbling steadily at its edges. So many families now own cars that parking is beginning to be a problem. Every young man seems to ride a motorcycle, and the lively dark-eyed boys dart everywhere on new bikes. Television is now virtually a domestic necessity. It is hard to take a picturesque holiday snap which does not include three or four aerials. We even an English-speaking parish priest. Father Athanasios has moved to a more prestigious position, and our new Papa Spiro worked for many years in Cardiff, before returning to his native island. He is regarded as very *'modernos'*, having been observed at work in his garden wearing shorts.

It is too soon to write about the roots that we are putting down, about the creative act of moulding a new house and garden and orange grove into a home where we and our children and grandchildren and friends can feel at peace, and about the neighbours who are also a part of our life. Maybe we have not yet reached our Ithaca. It is enough that on the long journey we have learned, as Cavafy said that we would, what Ithacas are all about.